SUPREME

&

JUSTICE

ERNEST MORRIS

Good2Go Publishing

Supreme & Justice
Written by Ernest Morris
Cover design: Davida Baldwin
Typesetter: Mychea
ISBN: 9781943686483
Copyright ©2017 Good2Go Publishing
Published 2017 by Good2Go Publishing
7311 W. Glass Lane • Laveen, AZ 85339
www.good2gopublishing.com
https://twitter.com/good2gobooks
G2G@good2gopublishing.com
www.facebook.com/good2gopublishing
www.instagram.com/good2gopublishing

ACKNOWLEDGEMENTS

First and foremost, I have to thank God once again for keeping me focused long enough to produce another novel.

Second, I would like to thank all my readers for supporting me and keeping me motivated to bring you into my world, whether it be fiction or nonfiction.

There are so many friends and family members to thank that I may forget, or would be writing forever, but if you have supported me in any way, I thank you.

Whether you have purchased a book, read someone else's book, recommended the book to someone, or even hated on the book, whatever the case may be, it's all good. Thank you!

Special thanks goes out to Good2Go Publishing for continuing to believe in me.

Thanks to my kids for staying focused in school, as well as life altogether. Thanks to my kids' mothers for being so strong and devoted.

I want to give a special shout-out to my homie Mattie Ice from GNS (Norristown PA). Keep ya head up, bro, you'll be home soon. Out of all the people I build with, you got the brains and potential to be something. It's a little bit of you in the characters. You are Supreme and Justice lol. Oh yeah, I almost forgot, if Gabrielle Gonzalez (from Camden, NJ) is reading this, Matt still loves you.

Shout out to Hassan Akbar, Footie, LS, Lex, Knowledge, Doe, Skin, Jay, Omar, Peanut, Mike Mike, Sheed, Feece, Lonnie, Triz, Peanut, Rafiq, Du, Whoopie, Mayo, etc. Anyone else that I forgot to mention, it wasn't intentional, but thank you also. I've done it again!!!!

DEDICATION

I dedicate this book to all the men and women just coming home, or that are on their way home from doing time in prison. It's a new day, and we need to cherish this opportunity because there may not be another.

You may feel that someone owes you something and your pride may get in the way, but think about where you came from and all the obstacles that you had to overcome. Use that as your motivation to take the necessary steps forward, instead of going backward.

Remember, for every action, there's a reaction, and for every reaction, there will always be consequences. What I'm saying is, don't come home with the same mentality that you went in with. It can only lead to two things: you going back to prison, or six feet under. Either way you will lose and they will win.

BE SAFE AND ENJOY FREEDOM!!!!!

SUPREME
&
JUSTICE

PROLOGUE

Spring of year 2000

"THIS PLACE IS BEAUTIFUL," Jade said, setting her bags down on the bed.

"I know. What are we going to do first?" Tina chimed in.

Tina, born Christina Thomas, was spoiled her whole life. Her father was a judge and her mother a councilwoman. After she graduated high school with honors, she went to Yale University for law school because she wanted to become a judge like her father. She never expected the college life to be as hard as it was. In her parents' eyes, she was a sweet and precious little girl, and she always tried to make them proud of her. She decided to go to Hawaii with two of her friends for a week's vacation. Her parents protested the idea because they thought she should be home studying. She convinced them that she would double up on her studying once she returned.

"I'm going to take a shower, then go get a tan on the beach, and maybe meet some hot guys," Brittany replied, heading into the bathroom. The loft they were staying in was huge and immaculate. It was Brittany's idea to go there instead of Florida, where all the other college kids go. After they took their showers, they headed out to the beach to enjoy the cool breeze near the ocean.

"What is that you're drinking?"

"Jamaican me happy."

"I want one of those," Jade smiled, tasting Brittany's drink.

"Tina, are you having fun? This is way better than Florida, isn't it?" Brittany asked her friend.

Tina tilted the sunglasses she was wearing. "Yes, I can definitely get used to coming here for spring vacation."

"Damn, look at those studs heading in our direction," Brittany whispered as two Hawaiian men approached the ladies.

"How are you ladies doing?" one of the men asked.

He wasn't wearing a shirt, which displayed his ripped-up abs. The girls couldn't help but stare a little too long. Even though he was good looking, Tina turned her head.

"We're good!" Tina replied, trying to act like she wasn't interested.

"I don't mean to disturb you, but we are having a little party in our room tonight. If y'all aren't too busy, you should come through."

"We'll think about it," Jade replied, already knowing that they would be attending whatever those handsome men were throwing.

"Okay, our lodge is right over there," the other dude pointed out. "You can wear whatever you like, just come."

"What is your name?"

"My name is Mateo, and this is Keo."

"I'm Jade, that's Brittany, and that's Christina, but we call her Tina," Jade said, shaking his hand.

"Well we have some things to take care of before the party, so hopefully we'll see you beautiful ladies later."

Mateo smiled as they walked off.

"We are definitely going, right?" Brittany blurted out.

"Hell yeah!" Jade said.

They finished enjoying the sun and the nice breeze that came from the ocean. Afterward they went back to their rooms to find something to wear to the party they were invited to. Jade and Brittany were more excited than Tina was. She just wanted to stay back and study for the exams coming up next week. She sucked up her pride and got dressed for the party, just so she could try to have fun with her friends.

~ ~ ~

When the girls arrived at the party, there was hardly anyone dancing. There were more guys than women, sitting around drinking and talking. Tina was not feeling the atmosphere and wanted to leave, but she had to find an excuse first. She decided to say she was feeling sick.

"I'm not feeling so good. I'm just going to go back to the room and lay down for awhile. Maybe if I feel better I'll come back."

"Okay, you know where we are if you need us," Brittany said, giving Tina a hug, then joining her friend at the table full of liquor.

"Have fun and try not to get too drunk," Tina yelled out.

She went back to their loft and read one of the books that she had brought along. It was an urban novel called *Naughty Housewives* by Ernest Morris. She loved reading when she was by herself. It was one of the remedies that relaxed her and took her away from reality. Not even an hour later, she was out like a light. What woke her up was the sound of moaning coming from somewhere in the room. When she looked over, both of her friends were having sex with the two Hawaiian men they met earlier. She had never seen her friends this bold or freaky.

"Would you like to join us?" Jade offered.

Tina declined the offer and acted like she was going back to sleep. She had always been a freak, but only when in a relationship. She had broken up with her boyfriend because she headed to Yale and he went off to Stanford. They both thought being in a long-distance relationship would only compromise everything. Honestly, Tina wanted to join in on the festivities, but couldn't conjure up enough courage to do so.

Their fun lasted for hours, and the whole-time Tina played with herself without them noticing. She had multiple orgasms as she imagined that it was her on the other bed with them. The two guys left out in the wee hours of the morning, leaving the ladies tired and satisfied. Jade mustered up enough strength to take a shower before dozing off to sleep. Brittany just washed up a little, deciding to take a shower later.

The next night, they decided to hang out with the same guys again at a local club. When they arrived, the guys had brought along a friend to keep Tina occupied. He resembled the actor "The Rock," same build and skin tone. The only difference between the two was that this guy had long jet-black hair that came down to his lower back, and a tribal tattoo that covered both of his muscular arms. The red thong Tina had on instantly got moist at the sight of the specimen standing before her. They all danced, drank, and talked until it was time for the club to close.

"How about a nightcap back at my place?" Mateo whispered in Jade's ear. "I have some friends coming over, and afterward we can repeat last night."

"How about we skip having another party at your place and have a private one at mine, minus your friends?" She smirked, rubbing his leg.

"Let's get out of here then."

They all headed back to the girls' place and had the time of their life. Tina even joined in on the fun, with a special request that the only one that could enter her was the Dwayne Johnson look-alike. They all ended up fucking, sucking, and everything that came with it the whole night. By the end of the week, they were exhausted from all the sex, drinking, and partying they did had done.

When they got on the plane, the girls slept for the whole

flight back to the States. After visiting their families, the girls met back up at school. Everything went back to normal for the most part. Two things changed on that trip though, that shy girl performance that Jade and Brittany used to portray went out the door, and Tina found out that she was pregnant. It had been a week and her period was late. She knew she had to tell her parents, but she didn't know how.

After thinking about her options, Tina finally broke down and told them. They were highly upset with her irresponsible acts. They gave her an ultimatum to either get an abortion or they would have nothing else to do with her. Tina's parents were very sensitive about what their peers would say if they found out that their daughter was conceiving a baby before marriage. They would be the laughing stocks of their community, and that's something they just couldn't have.

"I'm not killing my baby, Dad."

She thought it would be best to tell them in person, so she drove home after class to give them the news. Her father told her not to come back home and that they would no longer be paying her tuition. Sure enough, they cut her off of everything, leaving her to fend for herself.

Tina ended up leaving her college dorm and moving in with Jade's sister, Monica, who was into three things: girls, drugs, and clubbing. She was a rich white girl, living in Jacksonville, Florida. She inherited her riches from her parents who died in a plane crash on their way from Paris. She would let Monica have her way with her, in exchange for food, shelter, and other things. Tina was so used to getting everything she wanted, that once it was all taken away, she was lost.

By the time the twins were born in December of 2000, Tina was strung out on drugs. The twin boys looked exactly like the guy she had had sex with in Hawaii. Monica and Tina named them Supreme and Justice. Tina loved her kids so much, but loved getting high even more. It was Monica's fault that she got turned out.

One day she left out the house because she needed

money to get high. She and Monica had an argument because Monica wouldn't give her any of the drugs she had. Tina left the twins with Monica but never returned. Monica stopped getting high so she could take care of them. She taught them how to crawl, walk, and talk. As time went by, Supreme would always cry to be held and sung to, while Justice hardly shed a tear. Monica's money was starting to run thin, but she still tried her best to give Supreme and Justice everything they needed.

At the age of four, the twins started getting their own personalities. Supreme took a liking to all the ol' skool flicks, and would imitate them in his room. He would sit down for hours watching movies such as *Super Fly* and *Shaft*. He could recite everything they said word for word. Justice, on the other hand, was the quiet type. He liked watching action movies such as *Heat* and *King of New York*. His favorite of all time was *Scarface*.

"Get down here and eat, Just and Preme," Monica yelled upstairs, calling them by the nicknames she had given them.

"Yes, Auntie Monica! Here we come," Justice replied.

"Wash your dirty hands too!"

She fixed their plates, and they all sat down to eat dinner. Monica was a great cook. She made some butter steaks, mashed potatoes and gravy, and green beans. Supreme and Justice ate dinner, then headed back upstairs to take a shower. They were anxious to go to the mall in the morning with Monica. She was buying them something for their birthday. She treated them so well, and they loved her like a mother.

Later that night while everyone was in bed, Monica received a call from the hospital. Tina had been beaten, raped, and left for dead. Even though Tina had left Monica with the kids while she went out tricking to get high, Monica still loved her. She gathered the twins up and headed to the emergency room.

"I'm here to see Christina Thomas, please! They said she was in the ICU."

"Down the hall, first door on the right. You can check in

with the receptionist," the nurse replied, buzzing them in.

When Monica walked into the room, she broke down crying at the sight of her friend. She had broken ribs, lacerations all over, and her lips were like balloons. Tina told her that one of the local drug dealers did it to her because she didn't have the money she owed him. Monica felt like she was responsible for what happened to Tina. She took the kids back home and put them back in bed.

After making sure they were safely tucked in for the night, she went to her basement and removed her compact 9mm from the lockbox she had hidden. She changed into an all-black jumpsuit and then headed out to find the person responsible for her friend's condition. She knew exactly where to find him since she used to cop her drugs from him.

"Where's my fucking money?" Woop asked the fiend trying to score.

"I will bring your money when I get paid Friday."

"Come back when you have my money," he said, kicking the fiend in the ass.

Monica pulled up just as the fiend was walking off. Woop walked up to the passenger side and stuck his head inside the window.

"Long time no see! What do you want?" he asked, licking his lips.

Monica looked into his eyes, seeing nothing but a cold-hearted abuser, and pulled out her gun, aiming it at his head.

"Revenge!" she stated, pulling the trigger.

Bloca, bloca! The guns went off, and the two bullets hit Woop twice in the face.

Everyone on the block started running for cover, even the other dealers that were selling around the area. Brain matter spilled all over the passenger seat. Monica hurriedly pulled off and headed home. She rushed into the house, took a quick shower, and then fell asleep.

The next morning, she woke up to the loud banging at her door. When she looked out the window, the house was surrounded by police officers and SWAT teams. Monica ran into the twins' room and woke them up.

"No matter what happens to me I want y'all to know that I will always love you."

"Auntie, what's wrong?" Supreme asked, wiping his eyes and sitting up.

"I done a bad thing and have to go outside to talk to some people," she told them. "Whatever you hear, don't get out of bed."

She gave both of them a hug and kiss on the forehead, before leaving the room. Supreme listened, but Justice knew that something was wrong. He told Supreme to come on, and Justice followed his big brother (only by two minutes) to the living room. They looked out the window, and what they saw would change their lives forever. Monica was outside shooting at the cops. She promised herself that she would never end up in anybody's prison.

"Auntie Monica," Supreme cried out.

Justice just stood there and watched with so much hate in his heart for those cops, as Monica managed to kill two cops, before getting hit thirty-seven times by the rest of the force. The cops approached her body cautiously, making sure the threat was eliminated. They then stormed the house in search for anyone else they deemed to be a threat. When they came in, they found the two boys staring at them with hatred.

They took the boys and placed them in child protection until they could get in touch with a family member. Unbeknownst to any of them, Tina had gotten out of the hospital that morning and ended up overdosing. Since they didn't have a next of kin, they were shipped out of Florida and placed in a boys home. It didn't take long before the two boys were adopted. The problem was, they ended up going to two different families. Supreme was adopted by a white family that has an eleven-year-old daughter and lived in the middle-class area of Delaware. Justice was adopted by an old lady who took on kids for the money and lived in the Riverside Housing projects also in Delaware.

Welcome to Supreme Justice!!!

ONE

SUPREME SAT IN HIS room watching one of his favorite movies. His parents were out at work, so they had hired a girl from down the street to babysit him and his sister. Even though Elizabeth was three years older than him, he still acted like he was the big brother.

At the age of ten, Supreme was so handsome that whenever they were out, women and little girls had to speak to or touch him, especially his hair. It was so long that it came down his back. His parents had suggested that he cut it, but he declined the request.

"Supreme, Tara said come eat," Elizabeth shouted, barging into his room.

"I told you to call me Preme. Now get out of my room," he replied.

"Well, Preme, come eat," she told him again, leaving the

room.

Supreme laughed at his sister. He loved her because she worshiped the ground he walked on, and he enjoyed her company. They were very close and shared everything. He paused the DVD player and went downstairs to eat.

"I'm going to go outside and smoke a cigarette if you want me. Supreme, after you eat, go take your shower," Tara said, opening the back door.

"You better call him Preme before he gets mad," Elizabeth smirked.

"Whatever!" Tara replied, closing the door behind her.

She actually blushed thinking about how the little boy had the little girls fighting over him. Liz would tell her all about it when they came home from school. Even his female teachers had little crushes on him. He would never get in trouble, no matter what he did. None of the boys in school liked him because of all the attention he got. Some of them called him gay, until he poked one of them with a pencil.

"Liz, I'm taking my food in my room. Don't tell Tara,

okay?"

"I won't say anything! Can I watch TV with you later?"

"Sure!" he told her, heading to his room so he could finish watching *Superfly*.

As Supreme watched his DVD, he thought about his twin. His memories were faint because they were separated at a young age. His adoptive parents had tried to adopt Justice too, but someone else had already beaten them to it. Preme wondered if Justice still remembered him and if he would ever see him again. His thoughts were interrupted by a soft tap on his door.

"Come in," he said, already knowing who it was.

Elizabeth walked in, closing the door behind her. She jumped on the bed next to him. Just like all the girls in school, Elizabeth was in love with her adopted brother. They would play house, and she would always be his wife. At age thirteen, she knew about things that little kids her age shouldn't even be thinking about. She used to peak in her parents' room and watch them having sex. Preme was a little intimidated by her aggressiveness, but never showed it. She used to watch him take baths and would bust into his room when he was trying to get dressed. They watched movies until Tara made them go to bed.

"Elizabeth, it's time to get ready for bed. You two have school tomorrow," Tara said, opening the door. Supreme, you too, bed time!"

Preme wished he didn't have to go. He hated school and couldn't wait until he was old enough to cut class. Elizabeth left and went into her room. Supreme waited until Tara thought he was sleep, and then turned his movie back on. He wasn't worried about his parents because they didn't get off until eight in the morning.

Around eleven o'clock that night, Elizabeth couldn't sleep, so she put on her robe and snuck into Preme's room. Tara was knocked out on the couch, so Elizabeth wasn't worried about her. Supreme was watching his *Shaft* DVD.

"What did I tell you about coming in my room, Liz?" he said.

Without saying a word, she stood in front of the TV and turned it off. Preme quickly got mad at her for making him miss one of his favorite parts.

"What are you doing?" Elizabeth didn't even reply, she let her robe fall to the floor. Preme's first reaction was to cover his eyes with his blanket. "Stop playing and put your robe back on, Liz."

When he moved the blanket from his face, the look she had in her eyes informed him that this wasn't a game. Elizabeth yanked the blanket off of him and tossed it on the chair.

"Take your clothes off, Preme."

Preme looked at his sister like she was crazy. He was about to protest, but she began to help him out of his shirt. He actually thought they were about to play house. He stripped all the way down to his briefs. Elizabeth looked at her brother's body, noticing how much he had grown. He didn't look like he was ten years old; he looked more like seventeen. The little print in his underwear told her that he was growing up fast.

"Lay down on your back," she replied, pointing to the bed.

Not knowing what to expect, Preme did as instructed. Liz walked over to the edge of the bed and told him to open his legs. She stuck her hand inside his underwear and then pulled out his semi-erect penis. When her hand touched his flesh, he squirmed a little. She began stroking his manhood for a couple of minutes, then leaned her head down, placing him into her mouth. She started giving him oral just like she saw her mother do to her father plenty of times, not to mention the XXX videos that she snuck and watched.

Preme didn't know what his body was experiencing, but he knew it felt good. Out of reflex, he started moving his hips to her head going up and down. Elizabeth grabbed his balls, massaging them as she continued to deep throat his shaft. Preme had to close his eyes and grip the sheets because it was feeling so good to him.

"Stop, Liz, I have to pee," he moaned, thinking he had to

use the bathroom.

She never stopped though because she already knew what was happening. A few minutes later he pushed away from her and ran out of the room shaking.

"You just experienced your first orgasm," Liz said, following him into the bathroom. "Now you know how it feels when those girls want to do something with you."

Supreme tried to piss but couldn't. Instead, all that came out was clear white liquid. He thought that if what she just did to him felt that good, he wanted to do it again.

~ ~ ~

Since that encounter with his adoptive sister, Preme wanted oral sex all the time. He thought that it was the best thing that ever happened to him, and convinced the little girls at his school to perform those acts on him also. No matter how many times they tried it, none of them could compare to Elizabeth. It had been over two weeks since she had turned him out, and he was too young to be feeling that way, but he needed his sister's touch again.

Preme tried different tactics to bait her in. When she was taking a shower, he would act like he had to use the bathroom really bad just to be in there with her, but that didn't work. When their parents weren't home and Tara was occupied downstairs, he would try to walk around naked trying to make her horny and get her attention. That didn't work either! So he decided to fake a stomach ache, knocking on her door. Liz let him in, worried about him.

"What's wrong, Preme?"

"My stomach hurts so bad," he moaned, kneeling over.

"Why, what happened?" she asked, rubbing his back.

"I need my dick sucked," he smirked in a low voice.

"That's not funny!" Elizabeth smacked him in the back of his head and then pointed for him to get out of her room. "Don't play with me like that. We can't do this again, okay? You're my brother, and besides, I have a boyfriend now."

If looks could kill, Liz would have been ten feet under instead of six. This was probably the first time in Supreme's young life that someone had told him no. Everyone usually catered to the little boy because he was so handsome.

"Fuck you," he said to his sister, heading back to his room.

Supreme sat in his room that night and promised himself that no one would ever tell him no again. For the whole weekend he locked his door and watched different adult movies, learning about sex. He put a plan together in his head. Now all he had to do was execute it. When he went to school on Monday, he broke off any attachments he had with the little girls in his class that didn't want to perform the things he watched in those movies. They were so hurt emotionally that a few of them went to their teacher and told her what he tried to make them do. She immediately went to the principal, and they expelled him from that school.

"What the hell were you thinking about, Supreme?" Francis asked him.

"I want to know, where did you learn all this crazy shit from?" Larry questioned.

Larry and Francis were Supreme's adoptive parents.

Ever since taking him in, they treated him like he was their own. They provided him with everything he needed, and wondered what made him decide to do such a thing. Larry wanted to fuck his ten-year-old ass up, but chose otherwise.

"Well, we're waiting for an answer," Francis replied, sitting on the couch across from him.

Both of them had been forced to leave work early after receiving a call from the principal, and now they were trying to get answers. As much as Supreme wanted to put his sister under the bus, he chose not to. Instead he tried to blame it on social media.

"From TV and the Internet," he lied.

They tried to put him on punishment, but he somehow always found a way to still do whatever he wanted to do. After getting lectured for about an hour, he went up to his room pissed off at the girls who snitched on him.

"Are you okay?" Elizabeth asked, walking into his room.

"What do you want? It's all your fault that this happened. Because of you, I have to go to another school."

"Preme, I'm sorry! I don't want you to be mad at me."

He wasn't really mad at her, he just wanted her to think he was. They talked for a while and then she left his room. Supreme's infatuation with his sister had him doing things a normal ten-year-old wouldn't do. He watched different porn movies, trying to learn how to manipulate girls to do as he pleased. One of the women in the movie reminded him of Monica, and he turned it off. All of those memories from that night came rushing back. He still hated the cops for taking his auntie away.

"Auntie Monica, why did you let them take my brother away?" he said to himself lying across the bed.

Soon as he fell asleep, his twin brother popped into his mind, making him tear up. He always wondered if he thought about him and if they would ever see each other again. One morning he woke up in pain like somebody was beating him in his sleep. When he looked around, no one was there. Preme realized it was a dream, but deep down inside, he had a feeling it had something to do with Justice.

TWO

JUSTICE

JUSTICE WAS ADOPTED BY a lady with only one occupation, and that was trying to get over on the government. When she first laid eyes on him at the group home, Anna Mae, also known as Mom Mom, thought that he was so handsome. She immediately arranged to get custody of him. Once the approval papers were signed, she took him home to join the other adopted kids. There were three boys, including him, staying there, and they all shared the same room.

Anna Mae lived in the Riverside housing project. It was located on the East Side of Wilmington, Delaware. Poverty was at an all-time high, and the majority of the area was doing some type of drug. Justice could tell that Mom Mom really didn't care about their appearance by the clothes they wore. They were either too big or too small. She received them from the Salvation Army and other places that donate clothing.

"Go get dressed, Justice, so I can take you around the corner to get a haircut. My cousin's boyfriend is waiting for you," Anna Mae told him.

She hated the fact that he had longer hair than she did, and that was a no-no in her house. No son of hers was going to walk around looking like a little girl.

"No! I'm not cutting my hair, Mom Mom."

"Don't tell me what you're not gonna do. You have five seconds to take your ass upstairs and get ready," she yelled.

When he didn't move, she grabbed him and started whipping his ass. He tried to fight back but was no match for the 230-pound woman swinging the belt like she was possessed. After beating him, she locked him in the empty room that no one was using. She called it the dungeon. Anytime one of them got in trouble, they would end up in there. This was Justice's first time, but it wouldn't be his last.

"Let me out of here," he yelled, banging on the door.

"Until you're ready to cut your hair, you won't be eating

or drinking anything. I hope you like the dark," she replied, locking the door from the outside. "If you shit or piss on my floor, I'm going to make you eat it."

The room was dark, and the windows were all boarded up, making it so no light could get through. Justice went a full twenty-four hours without any food or water. He curled up in a corner of the room, and instead of crying, he thought of different ways to kill his adoptive mom. He was up to 221 when he heard the door opening. He stood up, expecting her to come back in swinging. Instead, it was his two adopted brothers.

"Here, hurry up and eat this before she comes back," TaJohn whispered, passing him two peanut butter and jelly sandwiches and a bottle of water.

"Thank you!" he said, taking the food and eating it quickly.

TaJohn and Chris had gone through this same ordeal countless times before, so they knew exactly what Justice was going through. Chris was the younger of the three but had been there the longest. Anna Mae adopted him a year after his mother went to prison for killing his father for cheating on her. TaJohn came about four months later, when his parents left him sitting outside of a police station because they didn't want him anymore. She loved the money she was getting from the state for the kids. If the state knew what she was doing to them, they would take them away.

"I tried to get you a cold water, but Mom Mom keeps track of them. She only lets us drink the tap water. Maybe we can get—"

"Shut up, Chris," TaJohn cut him off. "Hurry, she only went down the street to the store. She'll be back any minute. The only reason we didn't come earlier was because if she would have seen us, we would be joining you."

Justice quickly ate the food and drank the water. After he finished the food, Chris and TaJohn headed out of the room. Chris stopped before he got to the door, and looked back toward Justice.

"Your best bet is to cut your hair, because she will leave

you here until you do."

Justice watched as the door closed. He was now all alone again, thinking about what his adopted brother had said. He wondered how they tolerated the beatings and abuse that Mom Mom was so quick to hand out. He had a decision to make, and quick.

Forty minutes later, Anna Mae walked into the room with a smile on her face. She walked over to where he was now standing, then gripped him by the collar and leaned inches from his face. "Is your hardheaded ass ready to get your haircut?"

Justice didn't want to speak, because he was scared that if he opened his mouth, she would smell the sandwiches he ate not too long ago. He nodded his head yes, and she released the grip she had on him.

"TaJohn, take his ass over to get his haircut, and come straight back here," she demanded. "Y'all have an hour to get back, or you will be sorry."

~ ~ ~

"So, is Justice your real name?" TaJohn asked as they walked down the street.

"Yeah, why?"

"'Cause it don't sound like a real name. It sounds like a nickname or something."

"Do you have a nickname?"

TaJohn looked at his adopted brother and shook his head no. Justice stopped and looked him up and down momentarily.

"What?" TaJohn asked suspiciously.

"I'ma call you Tank," Justice blurted out.

"Tank?"

"Yeah, 'cause you're big as a tank," he said, causing them both to laugh.

"What about your nickname? You should have one too."

"Naw, I'm cool with Justice," he replied as they began walking again. "Anyway, did you like that name?"

"Yeah but just don't let Mom Mom hear you call me that. She will have a fit and try to lock you in the dungeon again."

Justice looked at his new brother and thought about Supreme, wondering if he was okay. He hoped that Supreme didn't have it as bad as he did, and wondered if they would ever see each other again.

"Fuck that bitch," Justice said.

They laughed all the way to the barbershop.

~ ~ ~

By the time they left the barbershop, Justice looked totally different. His hair was cut real low, and he looked even more handsome. All the little girls stared at him as they walked back home. He smiled, thinking that he was going to be the shit when they went back to school.

When Anna Mae saw Justice, she just continued watching television like he wasn't even there. "I want this house cleaned from top to bottom before I even think about feeding y'all trifling asses. Make sure that toilet gets scrubbed also," she told them.

The three boys cleaned every inch of the house starting with their room, so that they could eat. It didn't take them that long before they were eating the hotdogs and Ramen noodles Anna Mae had made for them. They ate everything on their plates and then played outside until it was time for bed. In the middle of the night, Anna Mae made them get up and clean the bathroom all over because she thought it was still dirty. Justice was pissed off but didn't say anything. His hatred for her would only get deeper in time.

~ ~ ~

On Monday, when Justice went to school, it was the best day he had since moving there. He was treated differently than before.

Tank had told him how to stay on Mom Mom's good side. Now he just listened to everything she said and never complained about anything. He made her feel like she was the best mother in the world.

In school Justice stayed to himself. Tank was in a higher grade than he was so they rarely saw each other, but they always walked home together. Since getting his haircut, he continuously brushed his hair until it was filled with waves.

He was always the smartest in class, and the boys there were jealous of him. They called him names such as teacher's pet or nerd because the teachers always showed him a lot of attention.

"Hey, nerd, can you do my work too? Maybe I'll get an A," one of his classmates said.

All the other kids started laughing at the joke. Justice didn't find it funny at all. He got up and walked over to his classmate. The whole classroom got quiet, anticipating what was about to take place. The teacher had her back turned, so she didn't know what was going on.

"How about you meet me after school and we'll see who's the teacher's pet," Justice said to him. He never liked the kid because all he did was pick on the weak.

"I'll be there!" the kid said, not one to back down from a fight.

For the rest of the day, Justice watched the clock, waiting for the day to be over. When the bell rang, the teacher dismissed the class. Everyone piled out of the building, onto the street, hoping to see a fight. Justice walked to the corner where he usually waited for his brother, and noticed a crowd forming. The kid he was supposed to fight and three other dudes started walking toward him. He dropped his book bag on the ground and then threw up his hands.

"So, he really wants to do this?" one of the kids said to his friend.

"He must not know that if he fights one of us, he has to fight us all," the other one replied.

Letting the group of boys know he wasn't scared, Justice pushed the kid with all the mouth and then started swinging on him. The bully stumbled backward and fell. Justice moved in, and was about to stomp the kid out, when one of his friends snuck him. The blow caught him right on the chin, knocking him to the ground also. He was already on one foot trying to kick their friend, so it didn't take much to drop him.

"Oh shit!" one of the onlookers screamed. "You just got knocked the fuck out."

Justice tried to get back up on his hands and knees, but the kid that punched him, kicked him in the face, causing him to flip on his back. He was dazed from the blow, and for a moment he didn't know where he was.

"Fuck him up," the kid that Justice stole yelled, getting up off the ground and heading toward the action.

Justice covered his face and balled up in the fetal position as the three boys began stomping him out. He was taking blows from every direction and then they suddenly stopped. When he looked up to see what had happened, his pain turned into joy. Tank was punching on two of the boys at the same time.

Justice tried to stand up, but his body was in so much pain. Out of the corner of his eye, he noticed the kid he knocked out approaching him with a glass bottle in his hand. Justice tried to move faster but couldn't because of the pain. He gave up and closed his eyes, preparing himself for the blow.

"Ahhhhhhhh!" There was a loud thud, followed by a

scream.

Justice opened his eyes just in time to see the kid lying on the ground out cold, with the bottle still in his hand. He noticed this Puerto Rican girl standing there holding a brick in her hand. She had two very long braids in her hair, and she was rocking a tennis skirt and a pair of all-white Converses.

"I couldn't let that happen to you. My popi always told me to follow my heart, and my heart told me to help you," she said walking over to where Justice was sitting. Her beauty was impeccable, and Justice was speechless. He fell in love with her at first sight. She was truly what a goddess was supposed to look like.

His trance was broken when Tank helped him up off the ground. "Come on, bro, let's get the hell out of here before the cops come," Tank said, helping him walk down the street. While Tank was helping him, Justice's head was turned in the direction of the girl who had come to his rescue. Their eyes were locked on each other until they were no longer in sight. It only made him that much more intrigued.

Since that fight, two things had been heavy on his mind: revenge and that Puerto Rican girl wearing that skirt. It had been a few weeks, and he still hadn't seen her yet. The boys that jumped him didn't look in his direction or come to class, but he knew that it was far from over. Since that day, Tank made sure to wait for him outside of the building instead of down the street where they used to meet.

"It's crazy, Tank, 'cause I feel like this thing with Kyree is still not over yet."

"What do you mean? That nigga knows what time it is, and I don't think he's that stupid," Tank replied as they walked home.

"I think he's just trying to let shit die down first." Even though Justice was young, he has been blessed with a strong intuition and always followed his heart. That was one of the things that made him feel connected with the Puerto Rican mommy who he still hadn't seen or found out her name.

"I think the shit is dead, but what are you trying to do?"

"I want to get him before he tries to get at me," Justice said, with fire in his eyes.

Tank had never seen his lil brother so determined to do something, but no matter what, he was going to ride with him. They walked around asking the neighborhood kids where Kyree lived. One of the girls that was infatuated with him gave him the information he needed, in exchange for him to be her boyfriend. He only agreed to do it so he could get what he wanted. He really only had eyes for one girl right now.

The girl told him that Kyree was staying on 22nd Street near Jefferson. Justice and Tank would walk past there hoping they would run into him, but he had been MIA. They later found out that his mother sent him down South to stay with his father because he was too much for her to handle. Justice still made sure that he kept his eyes open just in case Kyree's friends wanted to try something.

The girl that he made the promise to was named Gina. She had him by three years, and she was pretty. She was light skinned, had individual braids, and dressed fly as hell. Justice knew that he would need to get some new gear if he wanted to be on her level. Him and Tank stole a couple of pants and shirts from Foreman Mills. They didn't let Mom Mom see any of it though.

~ ~ ~

"Bro, you almost ready to leave? It's eight o'clock!" TaJohn said, walking into the bathroom.

Justice was looking in the mirror, brushing his hair. Ever since he got his waves, he would try to brush at least a thousand times a day. "Yeah, here I come now," he replied, never taking his eyes off the mirror.

When he walked into the kitchen, Anna Mae sat his plate with eggs and bacon on the table. He noticed that she had gotten her hair done. It wasn't nothing crazy, but he made her think that it was beautiful. "Mom Mom, your hair looks really nice. You look like Megan Good," Justice lied to her, making her blush a little. Anna Mae got so happy at the comment that she gave him five dollars for school. She figured that if he said something nice after all the ass whippings she had given him, there must be some truth to it. Justice took the money she gave him and hid it inside the slit he made in his mattress. That was the start of him saving his money.

Tank and Justice waited with TaJohn until he got on his school bus, and then they headed to school. "So, did you ever find out who that girl was that smacked bull with the brick? That's the type of person we need on our team. She's gangsta!" Tank said as they crossed the street.

"No, but I hope I see her again."

"You will! I'll see you after school. Don't get in no bullshit okay?" Tank smirked, heading to class.

Justice went to class, and everything went smooth and without a hitch. One thing was for sure, he still always thought about the Spanish mommy in the red skirt, and he knew she was destined to be his.

THREE

SUPREME

Summer of year 2014

WHEN SUPREME TURNED THIRTEEN, his main girl was seventeen. His birthday was coming up in December, and he would soon be fourteen years old. Kreasha turned him out with liquor, smoking loud, and skipping school. His adoptive parents thought he needed to see a therapist, due to what he experienced when he was younger, so they paid for one. Sometimes he would go, and other times he would spend that time getting high with friends.

Supreme was involved with a bunch of different girls, but only favored the ones that were sexually active. He spent most of his time with Kreasha, but when he wasn't with her, he was with one of the other girls. Since they were older than him, he learned a lot about sex. He was getting more pussy at thirteen than most of the older kids.

When Kreasha first met Supreme, she thought he was her

age because of his size and the way he carried himself. Supreme stood at five foot eight, 162 pounds, and looked more like he was seventeen. His hair had grown even longer, and you could see the Hawaiian resemblance all through him. She noticed how all the neighborhood girls gawked at him, and since the boys did the same thing to her, she thought they would be the perfect match.

One day Supreme was leaving Christiana Mall at the same time Kreasha was. When she approached him, she thought he was going to act nervous like most boys do, but nothing about him was nervous.

"Hey, if you don't mind me asking, what are you mixed with?" Kreasha said, stopping him outside of the Cheesecake Factory.

"It doesn't matter. What's up with you though?" Preme replied, not trying to answer any questions about his background.

He grabbed her by the hand and led her over to one of the benches. The way he took charge intrigued her even more.

"Ain't shit up but the money, why?"

"What you mean ain't nothing but the money? What you into?" Supreme asked.

"I work at McDonald's, boy! What you thought I was talking about?" she said, looking at him like he was insinuating something.

Kreasha looked good in that tight-fitted shirt and shorts she had on. Her shorts were so small you could see the blackness on the bottom of her ass cheeks. She had a pretty dark complexion, but her behind was so black that it looked blue. Supreme could tell that she worked out by the way her thighs looked. He thought she ran track or something.

"I was just messing with you." Preme smiled, playfully pushing her.

They sat and talked for a few minutes getting to know each other. When she asked how old he was, he didn't even lie to her because he knew she would still want him. He was just that confident about himself. Kreasha gave him her number as they waited for the bus. She thought about how she was going to mold this little thirteen-year-old into the man she wanted. Little did she know, he was already a player and was going to turn her out.

"Make sure you call me," she said, getting on the bus.

"I got you!"

After watching her bus leave, Preme stood there waiting for his. He sent her a text, giving her his number, and then called his friend to see if he was coming over to play Xbox with him. He thought about Kreasha's ass the whole way home.

"Yo, meet me at my house. I have to tell you about this girl I met."

"Is your sister going to be there?" Kev said.

"Naw, she went out with her friend."

"I'll come through later when my mom comes home. She doesn't want me to go anywhere until she gets off work."

"Alright," he stated ending the call.

~ ~ ~

Later that night, since Kev never showed up, Supreme called Kreasha, and they met up. She introduced him to the world of drugs. The first time he smoked some loud, he felt like that's what he was born to do. It made him feel even more confident than he already was.

"I have to go to the bathroom," Kreasha said, giving him a peck on the lips.

"I'll be right here," he replied, watching her walk off. He continued smoking the loud and watching *Love & Hip Hop* on the television.

"Preme, come here!" he heard Kreasha call out.

"Where are you?"

"In here," she yelled.

He wondered what she wanted as he headed toward her voice. When he entered the kitchen, he didn't see her. Then she called him again; this time her voice came from the bathroom. He walked over there. To his surprise, Kreasha was standing in the middle of the bathroom floor butt naked. Soapsuds covered her entire body, with the shower running steamy hot water, causing the room to be completely foggy.

"What's up?" he asked, feeling like he had a lump in his throat.

"Come here, I have to ask you something," she whispered.

Supreme had never seen a body so perfect since seeing his adoptive sister's. He walked toward her slowly, not knowing what to expect. Kreasha had her horny face on. "Ask me what?"

"Come in here. I don't want to yell it out to you."

When he stepped into the bathroom, she quickly kicked her leg up and closed the door with her foot. She kept her foot on the doorknob so he couldn't get out. All his thoughts had suddenly disappeared as she pinned his body against the wall. She had her legs wide open, and Preme could see her clean-shaven pussy. The pinkness of it had his dick at attention. Her clit was peeking out from between her tiny dark lips. He was still a virgin because he never really went all the way with a girl before.

"Wow! What do you want to ask me?" Supreme inquired with a high-pitched squeaky voice. For the first time in his young life, he was nervous.

"Come on," she begged.

"Come on what?"

"Aren't you ready for this?" Kreasha whispered, rubbing her pussy. Before Supreme could answer, she had taken her free hand, grabbed a handful of his dick, and started groping it.

"Oh, god that feels good," he moaned.

Kreasha leaned on him with all her weight, trying to rub her body against him. She dropped to her knees and started to tease him by gently nibbling on his dick through his jeans. The more she nibbled, the more excited he became. Supreme started feeling weak from her touch. She stood up and turned around, backing up on him. Kreasha rubbed her ass against him and then bent over and grabbed her ankles. After she was fully bent over, she started grinding her butt in a slow circular motion. "Take it if you want it," she said.

Her heavy breathing was turning him on. Supreme pulled his pants down and was about to enter her when he remembered that he didn't have any protection. He stopped abruptly and looked at Kreasha. "Do you have a condom for me?"

"Come on, baby, you don't need one," she moaned, stroking his manhood.

Supreme remembered all those movies he watched about girls getting pregnant, and knew he wasn't ready to get caught up in that life. He pulled his pants back up and told her that he was going to get a condom from the store.

"I'm horny now, Preme. Just pull out. Haven't you fucked without a rubber before?" she asked, disappointed.

"I'll be back! Don't worry, I'm going to beat that up."

He didn't want her to know that this was going to be his first time, but Kreasha already knew that it was. That's the reason she invited him over. Once she put it on him, she could control him, or so she thought. He rushed out to the store. Kreasha waited in her bedroom for him.

"I've been waiting for you," she said, fingering herself.

Supreme immediately stripped and then jumped into bed with her. They had sex for two long hours before Preme had to rush home. That was the night that a man was born.

~ ~ ~

"Mom, I'm going over to Kev's house for a while. I'll be back for dinner," Preme said, rushing out the door.

Supreme headed over to see Kreasha. Her mother had left for Florida, so she had the house to herself and wanted some company. When Supreme walked in, she was sitting on the couch with a blunt hanging from her mouth, wearing nothing but her bra and panties. He looked at the camel toe between her legs and got an instant erection.

"What took you so long?" she asked, letting the smoke flow freely from her lips.

"Shut up and pass that shit," he replied, sitting next to her on the couch.

They smoked a couple of Dutches before going into Kreasha's bedroom and having sex for a couple of hours.

Afterward, he headed home because he told his parents he would be back in time for dinner. Kreasha was pissed that he had to leave after having his way with her. She was supposed to be turning him out, but it ended up being the other way around. She had fallen in love with the thirteen-year-old boy.

Supreme's mom watched him as they sat at the table eating, and noticed how he devoured his food. Upon further observation, she realized that he was high off something, and snapped out on him.

"Are you out of your mind, Supreme? Larry, you need to talk to him right now," she demanded, looking at her husband.

"Supreme, come with me," he stated, excusing himself from the table.

They stepped outside so Larry could speak to Supreme away from the ladies. He wanted to explain to him the importance of why he shouldn't be using drugs. Supreme wasn't trying to hear none of that, but still acted like he was listening. Larry ended up grounding him for a week, and that didn't do anything but make him sneak out the house when everyone was asleep. They even tried taking his allowance away and stopped buying him expensive clothes, but that didn't work. Francis was getting worried because she thought she was losing her son to the streets. When they finally gave him his privileges back, everything was good until he started staying out too late and began smoking again.

Supreme even started blackmailing his adoptive sister. He told her that if she said anything, he would tell their parents what she did to him when he was little. That caused Elizabeth to keep her mouth shut and tolerate his destructive behavior. He snuck out one night to go over Kreasha's house, and was surprised to see her mother's car parked in the driveway. When he knocked on the door, her mother answered.

"Hello, Ms. Kim, is Kreasha home?"

"Not right now. She had to go take care of something for me. Would you like to come in and wait for her?"

"Sure!"

He watched her walking around in her tights, and could see the resemblance in the two. They could have been twins. Kimberly was happily married to Kreasha's father until he was killed over in Afghanistan, and their household hadn't been the same since. She became an emotional wreck and anti-social. Most of her days were spent at work or taking some kind of antidepressant medication that she had in the bathroom cabinet. It got so bad that she even resorted to using perks that she purchased from the local drug dealers.

Kreasha loved her father, but blamed his death on him. She thought that if he would have stayed home and protected her instead of the world, he would still be alive. Once he died, she tried to confide in her mom, but that didn't help. She then looked to older men to confide in, looking for that father figure, and they took advantage of her. Kreasha was very developed at the age of fifteen. She had 32C breasts, a twenty-seven-inch waistline, and a nice firm ass. The older guys treated her like she was a grown woman. They introduced her to sex, drugs, and everything else, and now she was teaching it to Supreme. She showed him how to please a woman with his touch, voice, and dick. Supreme was horny, just from the thought of what he would do to his girl's mom. He knew it would never happen though. Kreasha returned, and they went outside to the garage to smoke the loud he had brought.

"Your mom seems like she's cool," Preme stated, rubbing on Kreasha's behind.

"She has her days. I'm surprised she let you come in and wait for me. She must have thought you were one of my classmates. She's used to grown men knocking on my door asking for me."

"Well we have to hurry up before my parents notice I'm missing," he said, unbuttoning his pants.

"We can't fuck tonight because my mom might catch us. Instead I want you to do something for me, and I'll return the favor."

"What?" Preme asked, skeptical.

Kreasha walked over to one of the cars in the garage and

opened the back door. She lifted up her skirt, revealing that she wasn't wearing any panties, and then sat in the backseat. Preme watched her stick her finger inside her pussy and then stick it in her mouth.

"Come here!" Supreme walked over to Kreasha, thinking that he was about to get some. She leaned back on the seat, positioning her body so he could see her Love tunnel. "Eat my pussy, baby."

"What?"

"Eat my pussy! I'm going to show you how to do it."

At first he thought that was nasty and something he would never do, but he tried it anyway. When he saw how she reacted to it, he adapted to liking it. He pleased her for a few, and then she reciprocated the favor. It only lasted a while because Kreasha didn't want her mom to come out and catch them. Plus, he had to hurry back home.

The next day when he came to see her, Kreasha had invited a couple of her friends over for a threesome. Even they thought he was older than thirteen years old, Kreasha told them he was their age, and they had fun for hours. After months of learning how to please a woman's body and find her g-spot, Supreme became a master at sex. It got to the point where Kreasha and her friends were begging for Preme to fuck them. Most of all, he found out that his most powerful weapon was his tongue. It helped him talk his way out of anything, and was a girl's pleasing tool.

Supreme turned pussy eating into an art. His tongue was a paintbrush, and each pussy was his canvas. Besides that, he was learning something else also. The drug game! One of the older kids from around his way noticed how all the girls were on his dick, and was impressed. He asked Supreme to take a ride with him one day to pick something up. Supreme was infatuated with his car, and hopped in.

"Your name is Supreme, right?"

"No, it's Preme," he corrected him.

"My bad, lil homie. I see you chilling with all the shorties. How old are you?" Walid asked him, hopping on route 13, heading to New Castle, Delaware.

"I'm about to turn fourteen next month."

"Wow, you look like you're seventeen. You're starting young I see! That's what's up. You blow?"

"Hell yeah," he said, looking at the pineapple Dutch filled with loud. Preme could smell it all through the car before Walid even pulled it out.

"Spark, it up."

They smoked the loud until they pulled into an apartment complex right off of New Castle Ave, where Walid parked. They walked inside and met up with some dude.

"What's up with you?" the man said, shaking Walid's hand. He gave Supreme a look and then looked at Walid for confirmation.

"He's cool! What you needed to speak to me about?"

"I called you up here because I wanted you to see something." The man reached over and dropped something into Walid's hand. Supreme wondering what it was that he gave him. "Do you know anything about that?"

"It's raw dope," Walid said, wide-eyed, looking at the

off-white, egg-shaped rock. He had been selling dope for a while, but never knew that it came in that form.

"Can you do anything with this?" the man asked. "I have a lot of it, and I need to move it."

Walid paused for a moment, thinking about all the money he was sure to make off of it. He was gonna have to assemble a little squad of young boys to handle it. Just the rock he held in his hand was more than he had ever had, and he was about to get rich.

"Yeah, I can do something with it. I'm a hustler, I can move anything you give me."

"Are you sure?"

"Of course, I'm sure," Walid lied, not sure if he would be able to move all of it in a timely manner unless he got the help he needed.

"Well if you can move it, I have a quarter of a key that I will front you."

Walid's eyes stretched wide open. He started to calculate in his head how much he would make off of it. The man and

Preme both looked at him, waiting for a response. He didn't want to look so dumbfounded, so he just rolled with the punches.

"That's cool, I'll take it!"

"I will get the package to you in the morning. I don't want you to drive back with it, just in case you get pulled over driving without a license. Come with me so I can show you how to cut it. Your friend will have to wait here though."

"We'll be right back," Walid said, following the man to the basement.

Supreme sat down thinking about what he had just seen. He was amazed at what had just taken place and wondered if he could get money like Walid was. He used to see him counting money in his car as he walked to school and wondered how he got it. Now that he finally found out, he wanted to be a part of it. There was one problem: his parents would kill him.

FOUR

JUSTICE

JUSTICE HAD EARNED A name for himself amongst his peers, because he never backed down from a fight and all the girls were infatuated with him. Everyone thought he was soft because of his wavy hair and yellow skin, but he was far from sweet. He fought almost everybody in the neighborhood to prove his toughness and demand respect. He didn't win them all, but he won more than his share. That's why he was known as "the Kid with Hands."

He had just turned fourteen yesterday and wanted to celebrate, but Anna Mae didn't do birthday parties. He had saved only $175 in his mattress, which was a lot of money to him. It seemed like every time he would compliment Anna Mae on something, she would slide him a dollar or two. Basically, he had been hustling her and was good at it.

Anna Mae started acting more motherly because she finally got a boyfriend. His name was Malik, and he had just come home from doing twenty-five years upstate in PA. Justice wondered why he was messing with someone like Mom Mom, but he didn't know that she had been his pen pal. They met through Malik's cellmate three years ago and had been communicating ever since. She put money in his commissary fund and sent him urban novels like *Flipping Numbers*, *A Hustler's Dream*, and *Naughty Housewives*, by an author named Ernest Morris. She also came to visit him once a month. So, due to her loyalty, he promised himself that he would stick by her side.

"What's shaking, lil nigga?" Malik asked, standing outside the house.

"Nothing but this winter chill," Justice replied. "So, you did all that time behind those walls? I wasn't even born yet."

"Yeah, and it wasn't a cakewalk either. I'm never going back there. They will have to bury me before I see another prison cell."

"So, you rather be carried by six than judged by twelve?"

"That's about the size of it. Those muthafucking crackers

are the ones in charge up there. They tell you when to eat, sleep, and piss. There were so many times when I wanted to kill one of those assholes, but I kept my composure. If it wasn't for Anna, I wouldn't have shit, you dig?"

Justice nodded his head in agreement. They stood outside talking and getting to know each other. Tank or TaJohn never communicated with Malik like he did. They liked him, but they weren't as welcoming as Justice was. Malik saw something special in Justice that he didn't see in his adopted brothers. Malik knew this kid was going to be a leader. He just hoped that it was for a good cause. If it wasn't, this lil man was going to cause havoc somewhere.

"Man, it's freezing out here. I'm going in," Justice told Malik, opening the door.

"I'm going to put you under my wing and put you up on game if you're interested. If your gonna run these streets, you might as well know what to expect," Malik said, sitting at the table.

What Malik had to say piqued Justice's interest, so he sat

down at the table with him. Tank walked in to get a glass of water, and asked Justice if he was going with him to the store.

"Naw, you go ahead. I have to talk to Mr. Malik for a few minutes."

"Okay, I'll be back. I have to get Mom Mom cigarettes," Tank replied, walking out the door.

~ ~ ~

Over the next few months, Malik taught Justice about history, who the enemy was, and how to really defend himself. He used to be a Navy Seal until he was dishonorably discharged for beating someone to death with his bare hands in a bar fight. He had gotten so drunk that he lost control of himself after another man made a mistake and bumped into him. He thought Justice was too young to comprehend, but he soaked it in like a sponge. During the summer, Malik introduced him to his first hustle selling water ice and pretzels.

Malik knew a couple of people in the food vending

business, and they helped him obtain his business license when he was locked down. He was able to lease a stand, and placed it at the corner of the block. The only concern that they had was setting up in the projects. There were people that were surely going to try to rob them, but they would be ready.

"Whatever we make at the end of the week, we'll split the profits between me, you, and Anna. If we don't make no money, we can't split no money. You understand?"

"I do, but what about my brothers?" Justice asked.

"They don't have the fire that you have. Maybe if they show just a tab of what you represent, I will put them on."

One thing Justice didn't like, even if he was right, was people talking about his brothers. That made him work extra hard, so he could split his profit with them. Tank was a bit jealous of all the attention Justice was getting from Malik, but that all subsided because Justice shared everything with him no matter what.

In a month, Malik and Justice made a killing off the

stand. They were making so much money that Justice made Tank stay out there with him, just in case one of the neighborhood bullies wanted to try them. Justice stacked all his money except for what he spent on himself or his girlfriend. His mattress was full, so he had to hide it somewhere else.

Tank spent his money just as fast as he got it. When it touched the palm of his hand, it went into the palm of someone else's. His swagger was off the chain, and the women were starting to notice him now. He bought new clothes every week, and if he liked a girl, she also received a gift. Once the word got around that Tank liked spending money on women, it brought out the gold diggers.

"Bro, don't be treating those bitches if they're not doing anything for you," Justice said while they were counting their profit of the day.

"You must didn't see the way she rocked those jeans."

"Man, fuck all that. Once they see you grinding, they're gonna want to be with you regardless. If they know you gonna give it to them for free, they don't have to work for it."

Tank felt like he was the little brother the way Justice was dropping knowledge on him. He was definitely listening to him though.

"Let's go spend some money, Just."

"I'm still stacking my bread, and you should too."

"I'ma start next week after I get my school gear," Tank replied.

Justice could only laugh and agree with him at the same time. That summer made Justice and Tank the coolest kids in the projects. Everybody wanted to associate themselves with them in one way or another. Everything was great, but when the school year started, Justice found out just how much females weren't trustworthy. His girlfriend Gina's true colors started coming out, and she broke his little heart into a million pieces.

Gina liked everything about Justice, from his handsome face to his wavy hair. Since taking his virginity, they were inseparable. The only time you didn't see them together was in school or when he was working. When Gina started her senior year in high school, that's when she started to act like a totally different girl. The friends she hung with wanted to be around the college kids and go to the frat parties. They persuade her to tag along with them. The college boys would always hit on her, but she would turn them down.

Peer pressure was beginning to get to her, and when a few of her friends asked her to attend a party with them Friday, she agreed. Gina had lied to Justice about her whereabouts so he wouldn't know where she was going. The fancy cars and the way they just threw money around enticed her to sleep with one of the frat boys. That one time ended up turning into multiple times, with different guys. Soon they were tricking Gina out to all the frat boys, and she didn't mind 'cause she was benefiting from it: they paid for her services.

Justice was oblivious to what was going on, until one day Tank saw her getting out of the car with some dude. The guy passed her some money and then pulled off.

"That bitch got some good pussy," Tank heard another dude say that was standing in back of him.

"Who you talking about?"

"The bitch that just got out that car. We was at a party last week, and she was fucking all types of niggas for that paper. I even hit that pussy," he bragged. "She got some oils too!"

Tank couldn't believe what he was hearing and rushed home to let his brother know what was going on. At first Justice wasn't trying to hear that, but once he found out the truth, he was crushed. When he saw her later that day, she tried to act like everything was good, until he dropped the bombshell on her. She tried denying it, saying that everyone was jealous of them, but Justice wasn't buying it.

"I had big dreams for us, and you fucked everything up. I loved you, Gina," he said, with hurt all in his eyes.

"Baby, you're too young to be in love. You don't even know what love is. I'm about to go to college next year, so right now, I'm doing me."

Tired of the charades, she finally admitted it and didn't show any sign of a guilty conscience. His face turned from sorrow to a face with no sympathy.

"I wanted you to be my wife when I became rich and powerful. You gonna wish you kept your fucking legs closed," he stated, more as a promise than a threat.

As he walked back toward his house, he thought about what Malik had told him. Trust is definitely the cornerstone of a relationship, and he no longer trusted her. He vowed to never give his heart to another female. He meant every word, til one day after school when he was on his way home, there she was walking down Market Street. She went into the Cricket store with two other girls. He stood there wondering if his eyes were deceiving him. When they came out of the store, sure enough, it was her, the Puerto Rican that had saved him.

FIVE

SUPREME

SUPREME'S ADOPTIVE PARENTS WERE fed up with his behavior. He was failing school, didn't obey the rules at home, was starting to hang with drug dealers, and the weed smoking had gotten so bad that he was doing it in the house. His parents would get home and smell it in the air and then find roaches lying around everywhere. It was getting to the point where he was spiraling out of control, and it had to be dealt with.

When Supreme came home, he was exhausted from the all-night orgy he had with Kreasha and her friends. He could feel a lot of tension in the air when he walked into the living room. His adoptive parents sat on the couch with stern looks on their faces. He knew they were mad at him, so he tried to play the innocent role.

"Have a seat, Supreme. We need to talk to you," Larry said.

"Is everything okay? I'm really tired right now. Can we

do this later?"

"No, sit down and cut the bullshit."

Supreme blew out some hot air and then slouched in the chair across from Francis and Larry. They stared at him momentarily, before speaking.

"Baby, you know we love you like you're our own," Francis began. "But your behavior has been out of control for quite some time now. We aren't going to give you a chance to—"

"Dear," Larry tapped her hand, cutting her off. "Look, Supreme, you need help. You may not think you do, but you do, okay? We want you to see a psychologist, or you're going back to that group home. We're doing this for your own good, son."

Supreme stared at his parents with hatred in his eyes. Different shit was flooding his brain right now, and it was driving him crazy. He wished he had his own place so he wouldn't have to follow anybody's rules.

"I don't need to see a psychologist, Mom. I'm not crazy!"

"You need to talk to somebody, son," Larry said.

"Please, Supreme, we don't want you to leave, but there is no other option in the matter," Francis chimed in.

"Maybe you're right," Supreme said apologetically. "I do need help. I'm sorry for misbehaving and being a problem child. I promise to try, I mean, to do better."

"Okay, I'll call the doctor and schedule an appointment," Larry replied.

In his head, Supreme knew he had to be more discreet, and he promised himself that someway, somehow, he was going to move out of there. He felt like his adoptive parents had crossed the line when they threatened to send him back to the boys home. That was the ultimate betrayal to him. He thought they didn't love him anymore and were trying to get rid of him.

That following week Supreme started seeing his psychologist. Ms. Karen was one of those women that had insecurities about herself. She was very pretty, but overweight. She lived alone in a four-bedroom home, with her four cats. She hadn't had sex in two years, so every chance she got she bought sex toys and watched porn to pleasure herself. All her colleagues kept it professional when they were around her, but they called her anti-social and other things when she wasn't there. What they couldn't do was talk about her work ethics.

Karen was the best psychologist in her company. She dedicated all her time and energy to her clients, and had an impeccable reputation as a doctor. Karen looked over her schedule and noticed she had a new client. It was a fourteen-year-old black kid with disturbing behavior. She already had a plan to help him overcome his problems. While sitting there, her phone beeped, indicating an alert. She checked and saw that a new video just streamed on a porn site that she frequently watched. Karen closed her office door, turned the ringer off on the phone, and then sat at her desk. She hiked up her skirt and played with herself while watching the video. Supreme knocked once and then walked right into her office. What he saw, shocked him.

"Oh, I'm sorry! I'll come back later," he said, shutting the door.

Karen fixed her clothes and rushed out of the office after him. She spotted him near the elevator and motioned for him to come back. Supreme walked back to her office and took a seat in front of her desk. He couldn't get the image of her playing with her pussy, out of his mind. As she stared at the young man standing before her, she couldn't help but wonder if he was lying about his age. She had to check his file again, looking at his birth date to make sure. Her nipples were hard at the site of the handsome boy. She liked the way he was rocking his braids. They came down past his shoulders. "Are you mixed with something?" she asked.

"Yes, my dad wasn't black," he replied, but didn't go into details about it. He could remember Monica telling him when he was little that his father was from Hawaii. He even still thought about what happened to her right in front of him and his brother. That scene played over and over in his head. Supreme still hated cops because of what they did.

Karen offered him some cookies and chocolate milk that she kept in the refrigerator. Preme gladly accepted as she began the session. While he munched away on the snacks, Karen got lost in her own thoughts. She had her head propped up on her hands listening, but not listening to what Supreme was saying. He noticed the lust in her eyes and thought about how all the women and girls looked at him like that. Supreme decided to test the waters by slowly licking his lips at her. "Are you gonna stare at me the whole session, or give me advice?" Preme said, leaning back in his seat. "No! Let's get down to business. My name is Ms. Karen, and I will be your—"

"Can I call you Karen, 'cause you don't look old enough to have a Ms. in front of your name," he stated, cutting her off. Karen damn near had an orgasm from those words. No one had complimented her like that in a very long time.

"I guess there's no harm in that, and thank you for the compliment. You are something else," she replied, fanning herself with one of the folders on her desk.

Preme just smiled as he finished his snack and got done filling out all the paperwork she gave him when he first came in. Karen asked him about his childhood, and he told her bits and pieces, but not too much. While listening to him, she daydreamed about what it would feel like to be riding his face. She kept telling herself that he was only fourteen, but knew there wasn't any harm in thinking it.

"I will see you next week, Supreme. Try not to be late this time so that we'll have more time," she said, closing his folder.

"Later, Karen!"

He left her office with a smile on his face. On his way home, he formulated a plan in his head of how he was going to manipulate her into doing what he said. It was only a matter of time before she would be eating out the palm of his hand.

~ ~ ~

Every session they had, little by little, Supreme was seducing her. A month went by, and she was doing whatever he asked. Before leaving, he would ask her for what seemed like a friendly hug, but turned out to be him caressing her back. Within another month, Supreme began eating his therapist's pussy, and he had her right where he wanted. She was paying him to please her every time he came to a session. His sessions went from twice a week to four times.

~ ~ ~

"I want to get down with you," Preme told Walid when he saw him counting money one day.

"What you talking about, lil homie?"

"I'm talking about that," he stated, pointing to the money

in Walid's hand. "I've been saving money for a while now. I just want to get at a dollar like you. I can ride around with you and do whatever you need me to."

Walid needed a few soldiers on his team, so he decided to give him a chance. He told Supreme to take a ride with him to re-up.

"When we get inside, be cool, no matter what you see," Walid informed him as they headed inside his worker crib. Preme didn't respond, he just nodded in agreement. When they got inside, five other guys were there. All of them, including Walid's uncle, were walking around like zombies. They were bent over and scratching like flea-infested dogs. "They say when it makes them itch, that's a sign of good dope." Supreme smiled even though he didn't know what Walid was talking about. He followed Walid into the kitchen, where his uncle was sitting.

"What's up, Nephew?"

"What we look like, Unc?" Walid asked.

"Ask your boy over there," he said, pointing to one of the dudes that was zoned out.

"What's good, nigga?"

"Man!" he dragged on with a dry, aggravating voice. "We got a smoker!"

Both Walid and Supreme laughed. It was funny how he was slurring his words as he talked. He left out staggering, leaving Walid with a smile on his face.

"Come on, Nephew, let's get this shit bagged up. This shit is gonna go so fast," his uncle told him.

They began dumping the powder into the tiny envelopes. Supreme watched for a few minutes to see how it was done, and then joined in. It took them forever to bag up, and they still didn't finish. They ran out of envelopes before they ran out of dope. Walid was uneasy about letting the fiends help out, but his uncle insisted, thinking they would finish a lot faster. He said it would take the three of them a lifetime to finish. He knew they probably robbed him blind, but he needed the help. Their fingers were cramped from handling the little packets. They even ran through a whole box of masks because they were a must when bagging up pure dope. In total, they packaged 230 bricks, which equaled 11,500 bags of dope. Walid's uncle had stretched it a little bit, but it was still strong. One of the fiends said that on a scale of one to ten, it was an even ten.

"You have to leave me some," his uncle told him.

"You know I got you, Unc."

"Where's this going to be so I'll know where to go to get it? I have to let everybody know what you have here," one of the fiends asked.

"It'll be near the gas station on New Castle Ave."

"What's the name of your bags, so I can let them know."

"I don't have a name for it yet because I don't want to give it the same name as that garbage I was selling before," Walid said. "What do you think I should name it?"

"You asking me?" Supreme asked.

"Yeah, lil man! What you think?"

"Um, I would call it Lucifer."

"You heard him. I'm going to call it Lucifer! I need you to go to any supply store and get a rubber stamp made with that name. Get it in red letters so it will be easy to read, okay? Here is fifty dollars. Call me if you need more."

"I'm on it, Nephew."

"What do I owe your friends for the work they did?"

"Just give them a little something, but you have to

promise me a job when you need to cut some more. Is that a deal?" he asked.

"That's a deal," Walid answered. "Here!"

Walid tossed his uncle two bundles, and the rest he threw in the book bags he had. Supreme was feeling like everything was about to change for him. They headed over to Walid's brother house. That was where Walid was going to stash the work. He was going to keep it in his brother's basement until he needed to grab more.

~ ~ ~

Ever since he started hanging with Walid, Supreme started acting differently than he used to, and everyone was starting to notice it. His parents were watching him like a hawk, waiting to see if he was still fucking up or not. If his therapy didn't work, he was going to be sent back to that boys home. Since he was seducing the psychologist, she never gave him a negative report. It only made it that much easier to maneuver around.

"What are you doing today?" Kreasha asked, watching Supreme get dressed.

"I'm riding around with Walid today. We have some

business to take care of."

Supreme was walking around in a wifebeater and sweatpants. He just got out of the shower, after having sex with Kreasha, who was still lying in his bed naked. He snuck her in the house after his adoptive parents went to a charity event. To this day, every time he saw her naked, it took his breath away. She reminded him of that woman Porsha Stewart from *Housewives of Atlanta*. They had the same body type and features.

"How about one more round before we leave, daddy?" She blushed, opening her legs so that he could see her pussy lips poking out.

Supreme watched as she took her thumb and index finger, then began to rub her clit. Preme quickly walked over to the bed and dove headfirst in between her legs. He slowly slurped on her clit like he was sucking on a bottle. Kreasha pushed his head deeper into her as he flicked his tongue around her hole, sending chills through her body.

"Oh shit, baby, suck my pussy. Yesssssss, I'm about to cum," she blurted out.

When he started sucking on her lips and inner thighs at a

rapid pace, Kreasha reached her third climax. She suddenly wrapped her legs around his neck and squirted into his mouth. He enjoyed every minute of it. When Preme finished, he went into the bathroom to wash his face. He wanted to leave before his parents returned. He told them he was going to his session.

"What's up, lil homie?" Walid said when he and Kreasha got in the car.

"Ain't shit! Can we drop my girl off at her crib before we roll out?"

"Got you," Walid replied, jumping on the highway.

After dropping Kreasha off, they headed out to Wilmington to take care of some business. Walid had received word that some nigga named Pop was trying to move in on one of his blocks. This was going to be Supreme's chance to prove if he wanted to be part of the team or not. They waited for Pop to come out of his building before making a move.

"There he go right there, Preme," Walid whispered as they sat in the car and watched Pop walk into the building. "You know what to do, right?"

"I got this," Preme replied, waiting for Pop to come back out. Their wait wasn't long!

Walid knew that Pop wouldn't be alarmed by Preme's presence, mainly because he looked like an innocent kid. But in his case, looks were deceiving. Preme was trying to prove that he was ready for whatever. A person like that would kill in a moment's time just to be down. The fire in his eyes right now was the fire Walid saw when Preme first approached him. Upon seeing Pop coming out, he exited the vehicle and walked toward him. Pop noticed him coming in his direction and politely spoke.

"What's up, bro?"

"Shit. Just waiting on my mans to come scoop me up," Supreme replied.

"That's what's up!"

Noticing Pop not paying attention to his surroundings, Walid emerged from the side of the building. Still talking to Supreme, Pop opened his trunk to throw a bag inside. At that point, Preme pulled from his waistband the Glock 40 that Walid slid him a few minutes ago. He had never held a gun before in his life and was shaking uncontrollably.

"Get in the trunk," Preme spoke slowly.

Walking up to him, Walid saw a slight hesitation in Pop's actions and immediately took control of the situation. He took the gun from Preme and smacked Pop upside the head.

"Get the fuck in the trunk, bitch."

Hesitating is what cost him his life. Not one to repeat himself, Walid put a bullet in Pop's head and watched him slump over into the trunk.

"Hurry up and stuff the rest of his body in the trunk," Walid shouted to Preme.

Preme stood there frozen from what he had just witnessed. Memories of when Monica was killed by the police right in front of him and his twin brother, flashed through his mind. This was the second time he had seen someone murdered. He quickly snapped out of his trance when he saw Walid reacting.

Walid almost gave Pop another dome shot when a nerve made Pop's leg kick back outside the trunk. Quickly Preme helped Walid put the rest of the body inside and then shut the trunk. Walid poured gasoline all over and then set the

Benz on fire. They hopped in the car and sped off, leaving Pop and his car burning in the inferno.

~ ~ ~

Weeks had passed, and no one seemed to know what had happened to Pop. Many had their suspicions due to the fact that the car had been set ablaze with him in the trunk. The cops called it a drug deal gone bad. Supreme had nightmares about what happened that night, but never said anything. He fell asleep at Kreasha's house and woke up sweating. He had to go see Ms. Karen today, so he got himself together and headed to her office.

When he arrived, Karen was typing on her computer. She was wearing makeup and a shirt that showed off an ample amount of cleavage. Preme also noticed that she was even wearing perfume that smelled good. She was really trying to impress him, and the thought made him smile.

"So how is everything going, Mr. Smith?" she said, looking up at him.

"Not so good, Karen. I've been having nightmares about my auntie getting shot by those pigs," he lied. "I feel so alone, with no one to talk to."

"Preme, you can always talk to me. I'm here for you!"

"The only reason you're doing this is because it's your job. You don't care about me," Supreme replied.

"I know, Preme, but I love my job, so therefore I love helping you."

"So, do you love me, Karen?" he said, reeling her in for the kill.

Karen got so caught up in the moment that she forgot she was talking to a fourteen-year-old. He had a way of making everyone melt over him.

"I loved you since the first day I laid eyes on you. You are a very handsome young man, and I would do anything to make you happy. I don't care about losing my license over you, baby."

Supreme thought about Kreasha and what she would do if she found out that he was cheating on her. He knew that this was business not pleasure, and then walked around the desk to where Karen was sitting. Supreme leaned down and kissed her passionately on the lips, causing her panties to become moist instantly. Prison and losing her license were starting to become worth the passion she was feeling for this boy standing over her. She gripped his dick and started to caress it with her hand. He took her breath away each time he touched her. When he reached for her blouse and tried to rip it off, she stopped him.

"Hold on, baby, let me lock the door."

SIX

"HAPPY BIRTHDAY TO YOU, happy birthday to you . . ." the crowd of kids sang while Justice sat at the table smiling.

Today he turned fifteen years old, and this was the first party he had had since his auntie was shot down by the Jacksonville Police. Malik had talked Anna Mae into giving him the party, and she agreed as long as they were finished before seven o'clock. They also had to clean the house from top to bottom after it was over.

"Yo, you trying to smoke?" Tank asked, holding up the Dutch filled with loud.

"Fuck yeah, but not here. Mom Mom see us, and we're done," Justice stated. "Come on, let's walk to the store real quick. We can smoke over there."

"They won't know we're gone anyway, because they're all drunk," Chris joked.

The three boys walked over to the Chinese store and stood outside. They were laughing and joking when a tinted Lincoln Navigator pulled up. When the driver stepped out, they all stared at the jewelry he was wearing. This man was blinged out from the earrings he was wearing in his ear to the watch on his wrist. He walked into the store to grab something.

"That nigga is getting money," Tank stated.

"I'm trying to be flossing like that and drive a banging-ass truck. That shit is hot," Justice replied.

The guy walked out and hollered out to his friend in the car. Hearing the name, Justice looked over at the truck as the window came down. When he saw the person inside he could only laugh as she stepped out. It was Gina, and she looked sexy as hell rocking a short skirt with a tank top.

"Just get me a ice tea and a Snickers," she said, staring directly at Justice.

He was starting to finally see her for the gold digging bitch she truly was. He gave his brothers a nod, letting them know it was time to go.

"Don't worry about her, bro. Once you start getting money like that, she's gonna be on your dick," Chris told him. "I'm not worried about that bitch. M-O-B, money over bitches, is my motto," Justice smiled, giving them a dap. Justice wasn't as high as Tank and Chris were, but he was definitely feeling it. When they got back to the party, everyone was dancing and having fun. He leaned on the wall and watched. Out of the corner of his eye, he noticed someone approaching. It was the Puerto Rican girl and her friends. This time she was heading straight at him. Justice didn't know what to do, so he just tried to play it cool. She walked up on him but didn't say anything. "You not gonna speak?"

"Huh?" Justice replied, lost in his own thoughts.

"I said, you can't speak?"

Justice blinked twice and then looked her up and down. She was so beautiful to him that he was speechless. She stood there with her hands on her hips, waiting for a response.

"What's up? My fault, I was daydreaming." Justice was really caught up by her beauty. She stood at five foot one, with long hair that came to her lower back, and light gray eyes that looked like emeralds, and her body was impeccable. If it wasn't for her baby face, he would have thought she was twenty-one.

"I came here with my friends, but I didn't know it was your party. Happy birthday!" she said with a smile.

"Thank you! I haven't seen you since you saved my life," he lied. Truth was, the last time he saw her was when she came out of the store looking like a goddess. It didn't matter what she stepped out in, she still was a dime.

"I guess that makes me your Superwoman." She smiled at him.

"I guess so! Let's go outside and talk."

"Let me tell my friends that I'll be outside just in case they want me."

Justice stared at her ass as she walked away. She

whispered something to some brown skinned girl and then headed back toward Justice, walking past him. She turned and smiled. "You coming?"

He followed her outside, and they sat on the steps and talked. Even though it was December, it felt like it was spring time.

"So, what's your name, Superwoman?" Justice joked.

"My name is Gabrielle Maria Gonzalez, but all my friends call me Gabby. I'm Puerto Rican and Dominican, my favorite color is red, and I love reading. My friends think I talk too much because my mouth is always running. I've been in the States since I was five, and I go back home every summer—that's why you haven't seen me. Besides that, I love dancing and hanging out."

Justice was impressed by the girl sitting next to him. Something was causing his stomach to rumble. It wasn't from being hungry, because he ate so much food earlier. He had no idea that he had a case of catching the love bug.

"Well I'm Justice, and this is where I live," he stated,

with his arms outstretched. "I see you really like talking."

"Only to people I like, papi," she said with a smirk.

"So I guess you like me! That's good, 'cause I'm feeling you too. I just have one little thing that we need to talk about. I just broke up with my girlfriend, and I promised myself that I wouldn't go through that again. I just want to get to know you first before we get too involved."

"I feel the same way, only I wasn't in a relationship. Trust me, papi, I'm not asking you to put a ring on it yet," she said confidently.

Justice admired her boldness and the way she carried herself. They sat outside on the steps talking until Malik came out and told him that he had to help the boys clean up. He wanted to stay there with her, but knew better.

"I have to go, but can I get your number so I can call you?" he asked.

"Okay, but in a week, you will know everything about me and I will know everything about you. Is that a deal?" Gabby said, putting her number in his phone.

Justice smiled and said, "Okay!" He gave her a hug and then watched as she and the girls she came with walked up the block.

"We're almost done after we take the trash out and do the dishes," Chris said.

"So what's up with that Spanish girl?" Tank inquired.

He told Tank all about their conversation as they took the trash out to the dumpster. Tank could tell that he was feeling her. He just hoped that she didn't try to play him like the last bitch did.

"That's the reason you need to get money, 'cause she's gonna want things, and if you can't give it to her, she might want it from someone else."

"She not like that, bro."

"How do you know that? I'm just looking out for you, that's all. I think we should do that lick with my homie. We all can make some easy money off of it," Tank said.

Justice had money stashed in his mattress, but deep down he knew it was nowhere near what he needed. He was saving up to buy himself a car for his birthday, even though he didn't have a license. He learned how to drive by pretending in the backseat of the car, and through playing his video games.

"I don't know about that. What if we get caught or something happens to us?" Chris stated.

"Man, the fuck up and stop acting like a bitch. You don't have to go, but you better keep your mouth shut," Tank countered, getting in his face aggressively.

"Chill out, y'all! We're brothers, so we have to always stick together. I lost one brother, I'm not trying to lose another," Justice intervened. "Chris is right though, we have to be careful. Those niggas you hang with, Tank, is crazy, but I'm trying to get money, so what do we have to do to get down?"

"I'm going to hit him up and see if we can do something with them. Then maybe he can explain everything to us," Tank said.

Justice continued to stare at Tank, but he wasn't

listening. He was too busy thinking about Gabby and the conversation they had earlier. She really piqued his interest, and he couldn't wait to see her again.

"Justice, are you going with us tonight?" Chris repeated, snapping him out of his daydream.

"Yeah! What time are we going 'cause we have to be back before Mom Mom gets back from the casino."

"We'll definitely be back before then. She won't get back until three in the morning."

After they talked for a few more minutes and finished their chores, Justice went to his room to Facetime Gabby. They talked until both of them fell asleep. That was the first time he had slept with a smile on his face since the night he had sex with Gina.

~ ~ ~

It was now go time for the kids. They were about to hit a couple of drug dealers from out Philly that Tank's friend met a couple of weeks ago. It was supposed to be an easy lick that they would all come up off. They all piled up in Tank's friend's car and hopped on I-95. It only took them thirty minutes to get to Philly.

"Everybody ready?" Tank asked, taking a gun out of the bag and then passing it to Justice.

"Yeah, I been ready," Justice replied. He tried to act like he wasn't nervous, but it was written all over his face.

"Okay, here's how it's going to go down," Donte spoke up, taking control of the conversation. He turned the music off and then continued, "I want you to call Dominique. Find out if she still has that mark coming over to her crib as planned. If so, ask her what time we should be there." Dominique was one of the girls that Donte was fucking. He was relying on her to set up potential licks for his crew. At first there were only three of them, but now there were six. She had been part of the team since day one. Dominique was very sexy, which made it easy for her to manipulate anybody she wanted, man or woman. Standing at five foot six, 140 pounds, with long wavy black hair which she kept done, along with her nails and perfectly manicured toes, she stayed fresh to death. She was only seventeen and had seen a lot of niggas get caught up in her shenanigans.

"I'm calling right now," Bub said.

Everyone quieted down to hear.

"Hello!"

Of course, the only one that was about that life was Bub. Justice, Chris, and Tank had never even touched a gun until now. Justice saw firsthand what they were capable of doing though. Donte told everyone what they would be doing and how much time they had before they had to get out of there.

~ ~ ~

Dominique got ready for the company she was about to have. Her cell phone went off indicating that she had a text message. She read it and then replied, letting him know that the door was open and to come in. Next she texted Donte and told him that their mark was there. Dom checked herself in the mirror one last time and then smiled at her appearance. Walking out of the room in a short pair of pussy cutting Apple Bottom shorts with a matching wifebeater, Manolo heels, and her hair pulled back in a ponytail, she walked into the living room. He was sitting on the couch with his homie. He looked sexier than the first time she saw him. He definitely was making her pussy wet. Although her heart belonged to Donte, she still had her secret desires. If it came to her having to keep him occupied, she could probably give him some pussy.

"Hey, I wasn't expecting you to bring someone with you," she said, playing it cool.

"My bad," the dude replied, giving her a hug and squeezing her ass.

"Let me go put on something more appropriate. You can turn the game on if you want," Dom told him.

As soon as she closed her door, she texted Donte to inform him that it was two occupants instead of one. She waited to see what the reply would be so she would know what she had to do.

"Damn, she has a banging-ass body," Ty said.

"I told you that bitch was a dime," Cam said, grabbing

the remote to the 65" plasma TV that was mounted on the wall, and clicking it on. "After we leave here, we have to drop that work off at the trap house. We'll put the money in the safe at your spot."

Hearing all this from the other room made Dominique excited. They were going to come up on both money and work. This was going to be one of their biggest licks after all. She was glad Donte had brought some extra help, 'cause they may need it if shit got out of hand.

"What's taking so damn long?" Cam yelled into the other room.

Replying back with a smart-ass mouth Dom said, "I didn't know I was on a time clock, or that you was bringing someone to my house without letting me know."

"My bad, we just came back from handling some business, and I didn't want to travel alone. How about you make us something to eat, 'cause niggas is starving."

Dominique was smiling the whole time knowing what was about to happen to these clown-ass niggas. She walked out of the room and was all smiles, bringing them the Dutch filled with loud. After she passed it to Cam, he leaned back to admire her juicy, thick thighs and the camel-toe print that was poking out of her shorts that she never changed. "I'll be back," she stated, walking in the kitchen, knowing that both sets of eyes were following her ass as it shook from side to side naturally. She received a text informing her that they were at the door. She told him that a spare key was under the doormat just in case Cam or Ty had locked the door when they came in. Dom acted as if everything was good, bringing them something to drink. As soon as she was heading to the kitchen, the front door burst open. Coming in with the speed and agility of a leopard, four men ran in with their guns pointing at their prey. Not giving them a chance to realize what was going on, Donte smacked Cam upside the head with his Glock 40. The sound of Cam's flesh meeting his gun caused Ty to jump up and reach for his weapon. Justice quickly reacted, hitting him in the temple with the butt of his gun, knocking him out.

"Here, take my shit," Cam said, not sure what was going on, and thinking that it was just a petty robbery. "It's yours!" He held out the Rolex watch he had on without saying a single word. Tank punched him in the face, trying to get in on the action. Cam fell to the floor holding his jaw. Standing over him, gun in hand, Donte went to work duct taping him up hog style. Judging from the fear in Cam's eyes, it was clear he now understood this wasn't just a petty robbery. Scared to speak with all the weapons pointed at him, he chose to play it by ear, hoping that they didn't know shit while making a mental note of all their faces. He was definitely going to park each of them if he made it out of there alive.

"Raise your hands-on top of your head and roll onto the floor," Donte stated. "Lay on your fucking stomach, nigga."

It was clear to Cam that if he made any false moves, he would meet his maker. Seeing nothing but death in Donte's eyes, Cam thought it would be in his best interest to comply with his orders. He was just waiting for the opportunity to reach for his Glock 9 hidden in the small of his back. His hesitation cost him being smacked once again upside his head, rendering him unconscious. When he came to in what seemed like hours but was merely minutes, he was bound, gagged, and naked as the day he was born. Cam could only open one eye, the other was swollen shut. He tried looking around to see if he could find Ty, but he couldn't. He then tried to figure out where he was. It only took him a few seconds to realize he was on the floor in Dominique's room. He acted like he was still unconscious so that he could try to hear what the robbers' intentions were, but the sound of a wounded and desperate man squealing brought him to the realization that things would only get worse. His straining to hear what was being said in the other room was hindered by the increasingly loud pounding from the headache that seemed to be explosive. From what he could hear, he could tell Ty was being interrogated and viciously tortured. He knew he and Ty were going to die no matter what.

"Now I'm only going to repeat myself one time, and then you can move on to the afterlife," Donte screamed in Ty's ravaged face.

It took one hell of a man to endure the type of torture Ty was being subjected to, but after realizing he was a goner, he was ready to go out like a soldier. What he didn't know was death would have been a pleasant retreat compared to what was in store for him if he continued to not cooperate. In his current position, he was in bad shape. He lay asshole naked, legs spread apart as hot fish grease was being slowly poured onto his exposed genitals, making his eyes roll back in his head along with white foam seep out the sides of his duct-taped mouth. Justice and Chris were about to lose the food they ate earlier. Chris wished he had stayed in the car with Bub and kept an eye out for cops.

"He's ready to talk now. Take the tape off his mouth," Dominique said, holding the pot with the remains of the fish grease in it.

"Leave him in this tub to marinate for a while," Donte

replied. "Let's see if his partner will make better decisions. Matter of fact, Chris, you and Tank go check their car and see if the work is in it."

"Come on, bro!"

"Justice, come with me and Dom. Let's make that nigga talk."

With that said, they headed to the bedroom to see what Cam had to say. He was still passed out on the floor. They snatched him up and strapped him to the chair. Dom threw water in his face, waking him back up.

"Look, I spent the last twenty minutes dismantling your boy. His balls are gone, he has no fingers on his left hand, and he's missing his right ear, not to mention a few other things. I'm tired of fucking games, and I promise you this: neither one of y'all will leave here tonight, not ever. What I will do is this. Unlike your faggot-ass homie, you can go to hell without the agonizing suffering he's been through if you just tell me where the work is."

"Fuck you, pussy," Cam said and then spit in Donte's face.

"Go get Killer and bring him here. I haven't fed him in two days, I know he's hungry." Hearing this, Cam's eyes rolled into the back of his head. He had seen Dominique's dog when he first came through, and was scared as shit of it. He was a red nose pit bull that weighed ninety pounds. This was a huge pit and was very deadly. He shook his head, trying to signal with his eyes that he understood. His efforts were useless because no one paid any attention to him. Justice was even scared, hearing the dog viciously barking. Killer emerged through the door tugging and pulling on his leash and foaming at the mouth as Donte took his leash from Dom. Donte bent down trying to physically restrain the dog.

Tank came back in, and paused when he saw the pit. "There's a safe in the trunk. We brought it in the living room, but we need the code. That shit is heavy as hell, so there must be a lot of shit inside."

"I want the safe number right now," Donte said, looking at Cam.

Without waiting for a gesture or response, he let go of Killer. Attacking with such a ferocious and brutal assault,

Killer went straight for the kill, first tearing a portion of Cam's jaw off. He continued to bite any exposed body parts after Cam fell over in his chair. It wasn't long before the scene was a bloody mess. As big as Tank was, he threw up right on the floor. Stopping him before he killed Cam, all Dominique had to say was "Halt," and on command Killer stopped the assault and went to post up next to his master.

Standing over Cam's trembling body, observing the damage done, Donte told Dominique to bring a jug of cold water. Pouring the water on Cam to see the real damage done, he noticed a huge chunk of his nose was torn off, along with part of his jaw. Throwing more water and a towel to his face brought Cam out of his state of shock. Cam realized that he was really looking into the face of Lucifer himself. "It's 32-15-8," Cam mumbled through his half-mutilated mouth.

"Go make sure that it's right," Donte told Tank. "For your sake, it better be right." When Tank opened up the safe, his mouth dropped wide open. Dom came over to see what he was so mesmerized by, and smiled when she saw all the money and drugs.

"Jackpot!" she said, giving Tank a high five.

Tank went back in the room where Donte and Justice were and then gave him the thumbs-up, indicating that everything was there. Donte gave him a nod and then turned his attention back to Cam, who was hoping he would make it out of there alive.

"Let's do this," Donte said, rubbing his hands together. Knowing exactly what he meant, Dominique pulled out the Glock she had tucked in the small of her back and cocked it. Justice watched as she walked over to Cam, and without saying a word, shot him twice in the head. Justice couldn't believe how bold she was. She didn't even blink when his brains spilled out onto the floor.

"Take that, you bitch-ass nigga," she smirked.

"Damn," Donte said. "I wasn't done with that pussy motherfucker either. Especially after trying to play hard."

Next, they had to deal with Ty and then get up out of there. They walked into the bathroom where he was still squirming in pain. Donte reached for his gun, but Justice, seeing what Dom did a few minutes ago, wanted to prove to them that he was down for the cause. "I got it," he said, stepping up, aiming his gun at the badly beaten victim. He thought for a second about what he was getting ready to do. Then he looked at his brothers, who were now looking at him. He suddenly had a flashback of the night Monica was gunned down right in front of him and Supreme. He blacked out, and without hesitating, Justice pulled the trigger, shooting Ty in the chest and body area multiple times.

"That's enough, Justice, I think he's dead," Donte said jokingly.

When Justice came back to his senses, everyone was staring at him. It was like he all of a sudden had become possessed.

"Are you okay?" Tank asked, grabbing Justice's shoulder.

"Yeah, I'm good!"

"Let's get out of here before we have company. Burn this bitch down!" Donte replied, throwing the money in pillowcases. Tank and TaJohn poured the gasoline all over the rooms. Then once everyone was out, Tank lit the match and dropped it. The building was easily set ablaze.

"So, far no one reported any shots being fired," Bub said when they got inside the car. He turned the scanner down and sat it in the side of the door. "Did they play their part?"

"Those niggas got heart for real, especially Justice," Dominique stated, liking what she just witnessed firsthand.

"Yeah, they are part of the squad now," Donte added. "We are about to hit every spot in the city and take what we want."

As they drove down the street, Justice looked back at the burning building. This time he didn't feel like he was about to vomit, or anything else for that matter. All he could think about was when he would get another chance to bust his gun. That day was the making of a stone-cold killer, and he was about to wreak havoc on anyone in the way of his money.

SEVEN

SUPREME WOKE UP IN a cold sweat and looked around to see where he was. He had a bad feeling about something, but he didn't know what. He got out of the bed when he heard music coming from downstairs. His parents were out of town, so he knew it wasn't them. When he got to the bottom of the steps, Elizabeth was dancing with some dude, and there were three girls sitting on the couch talking to some other dude.

"What's going on down here, Liz? I'm trying to get some sleep."

"I'm just having a little get-together. Go back to your room and leave us alone," she replied.

Supreme walked into the kitchen to get something to drink, and then sat at the table and started eating an apple. One of the girls that was just conversing with the dude on the couch walked in with a smile on her face.

"Hey, want some of this?" she asked, holding the drink out to him.

"What is it?" Supreme replied, taking a sip.

"Just a lil something to get you right. Your sister told me that you're one of those bad boys that likes getting in trouble. Is that true?"

"It depends!"

"On?" she asked, standing next to him.

He could see that she was a bit tipsy and was being flirtatious. She was a white girl that never got in trouble, just like his sister. All of Elizabeth's friends liked him because of his good looks and because he was getting money since hanging with Walid. They thought that his mixed race and long hair was exotic. Elizabeth promised him that she wouldn't tell her parents what he was doing, as long as he didn't get locked up. Preme wasn't the type to back down from a challenge, and since this girl kind of reminded him of his adoptive sister, he wanted to see how far she was willing to go.

"Come here," he said, pulling her close to him. He stuck his hand up her skirt and grabbed her ass.

"What are you doing?" she moaned, grabbing the back of his neck.

"Just checking for something," he smiled, knowing that he had her. He pulled her panties to the side and then stuck his finger in her pussy, causing her juices to run down it. "That feels good, don't it?"

"Yesssssss," she replied with her eyes closed.

"Why don't you come up to my room and keep me company?"

Supreme started moving his finger faster, causing her to start shaking. She came all over his finger. He stood up and then placed her hand on his erection. She started massaging it through the sweatpants he was wearing. Just as they were about to walk upstairs, his phone rang.

"What's up, Walid?"

"Preme, I need you to take a ride with me to make this drop real quick."

"Where you at?"

"I'm about to pull up to your crib now. Come outside!"

"Cool!" Supreme said, disappointed that he wouldn't be able to knock shorty off right now. "Look, I have to make a run, but if you're still here when I get back, I'm gonna give you what you want."

She was sexually frustrated but didn't say anything. He rushed to his room and threw on his sneakers, and then walked outside just as Walid was pulling up.

"This won't take long at all. I'll have you back before your people know you're missing," Walid said as soon as Supreme closed the door.

Supreme was diving into the game blind as hell, and was getting schooled by a true vet. He was fifteen years old and was starting to see more money than niggas double his age. Now that one of their biggest competitors was out of the way, they were getting all the business.

"Chill, I was just about to knock one of my sister's friends down, that's all. Let's get this money first though.

How much he want?"

"A hundred bundles. We have shit on lock right now, and after we finish this, they want to front us a key of raw. I told them hell yeah, so we need to off this by the weekend."

"That's what's up! I'm with you," Supreme replied.

As they turned onto Frank's block, Preme began looking on porches to see if he saw him. He was looking on the passenger side, while Walid looked on the driver side.

"There he is!" Supreme shouted.

"Where?"

"Right there, three houses down," he pointed.

As soon as Preme said that, two police cars came speeding down the block. Then a third car followed. Walid got nervous at first, but the cops drove straight past them. Walid pulled over in front of the porch where Frank was standing. Frank dashed across the street and jumped in the car.

"What's up, fellas?" he asked.

Another cop car rode past, only this one wasn't speeding.

He was driving slowly, and then stopped when it got right beside them. Walid, playing it cool, nodded at him, and the officer nodded back at them. He gave them a look as if he had something to say.

"Is everything okay, officer?" Walid asked, showing that he wasn't intimidated by him.

Justice lifted up in his seat trying not to look too suspicious. Frank also acted like they were about to take him somewhere.

"Yes, I'm just making sure you guys are staying out of trouble."

"We came to pick up my cousin so we can go to my mom's birthday party," Walid lied.

"Okay, have a nice day, fellas," the officer said. He pulled off heading in the same direction as the other cops.

"I told you it's always hot as hell out here," Frank said.

"Yo, next time we're gonna have to find a better meeting place."

"Alright!" Frank replied. "Yo, let me go and put that shit

up before they come back through here."

Walid gave Supreme a head nod, and he passed Frank a ziplock bag filled with heroin. Frank smiled and then tucked the bag under his shirt.

"I want the same amount we discussed when we talked before."

"Alright, I'll be right back!" he shouted, getting out of the car. He dashed back across the street and into the house.

"Bro, this area hot as hell. We need to hurry up and get the fuck from around here."

"Shit, I'm scared as hell out here," Walid stated.

"You and me both."

They both laughed it off but continued to check their surroundings as they waited for Frank to bring them the money for the work.

"This motherfucker is taking a long-ass time!" Walid said, looking at the crib Frank went into a few minutes ago.

"Shit, he probably has to count the money," said Supreme. "That could take forever with this dumb-ass nigga!

I hope my sister's friend is still there when I get back."

"She probably drunk as hell, laying in your bed," Walid joked.

Supreme just smirked at the comment. He hoped that wasn't the case, 'cause if Kreasha came there and found another woman in his bed, it would be on, and not in a good way either. They sat there impatiently for about ten minutes, waiting on Frank.

"Come the fuck on!" Supreme shouted.

"Beep! Beep! Beep!" Walid beeped his horn, trying to get Frank's attention while looking over at the house. Five more minutes passed by and he honked his horn again. "Beep! Beep! Beep!"

Walid busted a U-turn to the opposite side of the street. They sat there for a few more minutes wondering where the hell Frank was.

"I'm about to go knock on that nigga's door," Supreme said.

"Here, take this with you," Walid said, passing him the

gun.

Supreme got out and slammed the door behind him, tucking the gun into his waistband. As he walked up the steps, he debated which doorbell to ring. The first floor had a name that was scratched out, so he rang the second-floor bell. When no one answered, he rang it two more times, still no answer. Supreme turned the doorknob, and the door immediately opened. He walked inside and looked around. The hallway was a mess. He stepped over the junk that was in his way, in search of the door he was looking for. He knocked lightly on the door, but no one answered.

"Yo, Frank, are you in there?" he shouted, putting his ear to the door, trying to listen for any sign of noise.

When he didn't hear anything, he tried to turn the doorknob, but it was locked. Supreme thought that he couldn't hear him, so he yelled louder.

"Frank, what's up?"

Thinking he was in one of the apartments upstairs, Supreme jumped over the first three steps and then skipped every other one until he was at the top. There was so much trash and junk at the top of the staircase that it was impossible for him to get to the door. The stinking smell of piss filled the air, causing him to cover his nose. Something didn't feel right to him, so he went back down the stairs. When he got to the porch, Walid was standing there waiting.

"What happened? You get the money from that clown?"

"No, you sure that was the house?" Supreme asked ignorantly. "Let's go around the back and see if he's there!"

They walked to the back of the alleyway in search of Frank. There was so much junk that they couldn't get through that way. Stoves, dressers, and refrigerators were blocking the path. Walid suddenly ran to the other side, followed by Supreme. When they reached the other side and looked up, there was not a window on the whole house. Walid peaked through the first-floor window. The smell of newly burned wood filled his nostrils. He ran up the stairs and turned the doorknob. It opened right up! When he looked around, there was nothing there. No furniture, no clothes, no sign of life whatsoever. The whole place was abandoned.

"What the fuck?" Supreme stated, walking up behind him. He glanced around the empty apartment. "Are you sure this is the house he came in?"

"I think we've been played, bro. I'm going to kill that pussy when I see him."

They headed back to the car and got out of that neighborhood before they got pulled over and their guns were found. Neither one of them said anything the whole ride back to Supreme's crib.

"Tomorrow we look for that thief and put him to sleep."

"Say no more!" Supreme replied, handing the gun back.

EIGHT

JUSTICE

JUSTICE AND GABBY HAD been spending a lot of time together lately. Every time he wasn't with his crew, he was with her. She had to go back to Puerto Rico because her great grandmother was sick and she requested that all of her family be present. They didn't know if it would be her last days or not. Justice talked to her every chance he got. He couldn't wait for her to return, because they were planning to finally have sex. He had been creeping around with random chicks until she was ready. He was sitting in his room talking to Tank and Chris about the next lick that Dominique had set up for them, when he received an unexpected phone call.

"Hello, who this?" he answered, not recognizing the number.

"It's me, Justice. Gina!"

"What do you want?" he asked, uninterested in what she had to say.

"I just wanted to say that I'm sorry for what I did. I know you probably hate me, and I don't blame you. Can I just ask for one last favor and I'll leave you alone?" she asked in her sexiest voice.

"I'm listening!" Justice replied.

"Well, can you please come scratch my itch? My pussy's on fire, and I need you to come put it out. Please, Justice!" she said, more begging than asking.

As much as he hated her guts right now, he did want to hit that one more time, and figured why not, since he wasn't doing anything.

"Where are you?"

"Home!"

"Isn't your mom there?" he asked.

"She's not here. She went to a bingo game with her friends again. You know she's never home, so can you come?" Gina asked again.

"What about that nigga you been stunting with?" Justice asked sarcastically.

"Justice, he had to take a trip. I'm only asking you to come fuck this pussy one more time for old time's sake. I'll never ask you to do it again if you want," she said.

"I'll be there in a few minutes. I'm about to call for an Uber ride now. You just keep that pussy warm for me," he said, ending the call before she responded.

~ ~ ~

Justice arrived at her crib about forty-five minutes later. He couldn't wait until he had his own ride to get around in. When he walked into Gina's house, he headed straight to her room. He immediately stripped off his clothes, not wanting to waste any time. Gina lay back watching with a glow in her eyes that said she couldn't wait for that hard dick standing in front of her to be inside her wet walls.

Justice had to admit to himself that she looked good lying on the bed, spread eagle with a finger already playing with her pussy. Walking over to the bed, he stood there for a few seconds, watching the freak show that enticed him even more.

"Are you gonna stand there and watch, or join me?" Gina asked, licking her own juices from her finger.

"Bitch, get on your knees," he said, looking her in the eyes.

She had never heard him talk to her like that, and was completely turned on. Immediately stopping her masturbation, she grabbed his dick and lifted it up, gently jacking it off. Knowing that it drove him crazy, she blew on the tip of it and then bent down to suck his nut sack. She then licked from the bottom of his dick to the head. Gina tasted the precum that leaked from the tip of his manhood, and began devouring it, deepthroating it while he grabbed her hair and literally fucked her mouth.

"Goddamn, that shit feels so good," he moaned. Feeling like he was about to bust, he pulled out her mouth, trying to let the pressure go back down. "Lay down on your fucking back!"

Gina lay on her back as he placed her legs on his shoulders and slid his dick into her dripping wet pussy. Not bothering to be gentle, he forcefully rammed his dick in and out of her, trying to knock the lining out of her pussy.

"Yessssss, baby, beat this pussy up," she moaned in pure ecstasy while kissing on his neck.

Pulling back, Justice leaned his head up so she didn't leave any passion marks on his neck. Then he started sucking in between her manicured toes, licking and kissing the top of each toe. Knowing he was about to cum, he pulled out and shot his load all over her feet. Still feeling her orgasm, she continued to rub her clit until she released her own. Satisfied, Gina hoped that he dripped some of his cum in her, believing in her sick little mind that this would bring him back to her and he would forgive her for the way she had dissed him.

"Where are you going?" she asked, watching him get dressed.

"I have to go. There are some things I need to take care of tonight."

"Damn, could I at least get some more dick before you just up and leave?" she asked with an attitude.

"Beep! Beep!"

"Sorry, that's my ride. Hit me up some other time," he stated, walking out the door.

Gina was pissed that he acted all funny toward her. Even though she was mad, she was still horny, so she pulled out one of her toys and went to work on her vagina. She had three more orgasms before falling asleep.

~ ~ ~

After talking with Donte, Dominique decided to call the dude she met at the strip club. Justice, Tank, and Chris were sitting on the couch, talking about how they were gonna spend the money they were making off the licks. Mom Mom didn't have a clue what her adopted children were up to at night. When Justice told Malik, he just said to be careful. He was kind of disappointed at first because he thought they were doing good selling water ice and pretzels, but at the end of the day, they were men. Once they got a taste of that easy money, nothing was going to stop it.

"Hello! Can I speak with Footie?" Dominique said into

the cell phone.

"Who's this?" the dude asked.

"This is Deja," she said, using the fake name that she had given him. "I met you at the Gold Club the other night."

"Oh yeah, lil momma with the huge ass," he said, smiling as he recalled her sexy ass.

"Anyway, do you still need some girls for the party, or are you straight?"

"If you have them, then most definitely. We don't want no shy or scary bitches though. We want people that want to get at this money, feel me? This is going to be my nigga's coming home party, so if they're not trying to get down and do whatever for that paper, then leave their asses home."

"I feel you, but my bitches are down for whatever, long as that paper is right," Dominique reassured him.

"That's what I'm talking about then, baby," Footie replied.

"So what's the address and the time y'all going to be ready for us?" After getting all the necessary info, she finished the conversation she was having with him. "Make sure you save your dollars because I have a special surprise just for you. I'm gonna show you how a real bitch gets down for that cash."

"I can't wait to see that. I hope you can back that shit you talking up," he said, grabbing his dick.

Dominique laughed at his cocky ass. She got off the phone thinking to herself, "If this nigga only knew."

"It's set y'all!" she said, looking at the crew. "The party is at the Red Roof Inn right off of 273. Bull's name is Footie, and he said to bring at least five bitches. He throwing a coming home party for his man, and from what I'm getting from it, they want to trick all night. When I met them at the club, they were throwing bread around like it was nothing. My guess is tonight will be no different."

"Well let's slay their asses for everything they got," Bub stated.

"I'm ready!" Justice said, cocking his gun back.

Tank and Chris looked at their brother like they didn't

know who he was anymore. Ever since he caught that body, he was eager to lay something down, and he didn't care who it was.

"Okay, Dom you take care of assembling the women for the show. Make sure none of them are your friends and they're expendable. Don't tell them anything they don't need to know. I wouldn't even give them the location, just that it's a bachelor party. We don't want them knowing about their one-way ticket to hell," Donte boasted.

"Okay, baby, I'm on it! I know just where to look," Dom replied, leaving the room to handle her business.

"Yo, the cops are still over at that spot where we lit up those bodies. We should have gotten rid of them another way, preferably using that lye we always use," Bub stated.

"I was just trying to make a statement, but you're right, we should have done it right. From now on, we do everything discreet," Donte said to the whole group.

"Okay, do y'all want me to drop y'all off at home?" Donte asked Justice.

"What time do we need to be back here?"

"In a couple of hours!"

"We're chilling then. Ain't no need to go home, then have to come back," Tank said, sitting on the couch with Chris playing PlayStation.

"Okay, I'm gonna take a quick nap so I will be focused," Donte told them.

He headed upstairs leaving everybody else downstairs enjoying themselves. It would be going down in a couple of hours, and this would be another big one hopefully.

NINE

SUPREME

SUPREME AND WALID RODE around looking for Frank for almost three hours. Every twenty minutes they would go back through the block where they met, to see if he returned. He got over on the wrong people, and they were going to get him.

"I hope that pussy doesn't think he got away with our shit," Supreme stated.

"When we catch him, I'm gonna cut his dick off and shove it down his throat, right before I blow his fucking head off. Nobody plays me like that," Walid replied.

"Fuck him right now. Let's go get this money."

They headed over to see Cash. They gave him some work the other day, and he told them to come pick some money up. Walid had about three blocks in Delaware and a bunch in Philly. Since Supreme was now his right-hand man, they were also his blocks. Cash had like five little niggas out there pumping for him, so at no time did he have to stand on a corner. They were all out there doing their thing thanks to Walid and Supreme supplying them. As long as that money came up right, Walid didn't care who he had out there. Preme had proved that he could handle himself even though he was only fifteen. That's why Walid wanted him to run Delaware while he ran Philly.

When they turned on the block, they had to admit that the block was jumping. There was so much traffic coming through that it looked like they were in the free cheese line.

"He should be almost done with the work," Preme said as they parked in front of the door.

"Grab some out the back just in case."

Cash was sitting on the porch in the middle of the block, watching everything. When he saw them pull up, he ran in the crib to grab the money. When he came back out, they were standing by the car.

"Preme, don't say shit about Frank," Walid instructed. "We gonna handle that nigga ourselves."

"Come on, Lid, you should know me better than that," Supreme replied.

"What's up, Preme and Walid?" Cash said, getting in the backseat. "I thought you wasn't coming until tomorrow."

"What's up, homie? I thought we would drop by now since we were in the area. What you got for me now?" Supreme asked, getting right down to business.

"This is most of it right here. I have a little bit more to get rid of, then I will be ready for you. If you want, I'll take the new shit now, then you can come back through tomorrow to pick up the balance from the last drop. I would have been done if it wasn't for the cops being out here for two hours."

"Is the block that hot?" Walid asked, passing him more work.

"Nah, some nigga was fucking his bitch up in the middle of the street, and someone called the cops," Cash replied. "They locked his dumb ass up. Anyway, they love this dope man. People from all over is coming through here asking for it. If the label doesn't say Lucifer, they don't want it. I was thinking about setting up shop over on Jefferson Street. Them niggas got garbage over there, and my man is ready to run through that shit and shut it down."

"That's up to Preme. He's the one that will be running this shit until I get back. I have to go out of town for a week or so," Walid told him.

Cash's eyes kind of lit up at the thought of this young bull trying to run shit. If he thought he was going to get over on Supreme, he had another thing coming. He would lay him down instantly at the first sign of deception.

"Oh, okay! Well what do you think, lil homie?" Cash said.

"Let me get back to you on that. Right now, I need you to get the rest of my money, and then we can talk," Supreme replied.

Walid nodded his head in agreement. He knew his lil man was ready to run the operation. Ever since he first introduced him to the game, he knew he was a natural. When he proved that he wasn't scared to pop off, that only solidified his worth.

"Well I will see you guys later," Cash said, exiting the car.

"You ready for this, Preme?" Walid asked, pulling off into traffic.

"I was born ready!"

"Okay, we have to make a quick stop to pick up something after we check out the last two trap houses. Then we'll head back. You drive so I can relax," Walid said, pulling into the gas station.

Supreme had driven his car before, so he was more than happy to drive. Plus, he liked showing off to the girls around his way. When he drove down the block, they would stare at him because he was driving and didn't have a license. Supreme couldn't wait til his birthday, so he could get his Ls.

~ ~ ~

It took them about two hours to pick up all the money from the houses and drop off the new work.

"Pull up behind that car right there!" Walid said, pointing to the Toyota Camry. Supreme parked in back of it, waiting to see why they stopped. "You like that?"

"Yeah, it's okay!" Preme replied, looking at the black car in front of them.

"Good, because that's yours."

"What?"

Walid tossed him a set of keys, then pulled out some papers from the glove compartment and handed them to him. "That's your new whip right there, so you can check on the spots. Take it for a spin, and I'll hit you up later," Walid told him.

"Thanks, homie," Supreme said, excited. He finally had his own vehicle to move around freely in.

"You still have to get your license, Preme, so those pigs don't try to harass you. Whatever you do, never keep the work inside the car, like we do now. Put that shit in the trunk, or get a stash box installed."

Supreme nodded in agreement, then gave his partner a

pound before jumping out the car. He got inside the Toyota and drove off. Instead of parking on his block, he parked around the corner so his adoptive mom didn't see it. She would flip out if she saw him driving. He walked into the house and rushed to his room to count his money. "Preme, what you doing?"

"Nothing, why, what's up?"

"Can I come in?" Elizabeth asked.

"Hold on a sec," he said, throwing the money in a shoebox, then hiding it in the closet. He opened the door to let his sister in.

"What's up, Liz? I was kind of busy."

"Preme, you don't have to hide anything from me. I know what you do. Everybody in school talks about you hanging with that dude Walid. I just want you to be careful out there, and don't worry, I'm not gonna say anything to Mom and Dad."

Supreme studied his sister's demeanor for a minute, trying to see if she was lying. He could tell she wasn't, so he let his guard down just a bit. "Thanks, Sis, now let me get back to what I was doing."

"Oh yeah," Liz said, turning around before walking out the door, "my friend said you owe her, and she wants it when she comes over tomorrow."

Supreme smiled, thinking about what he didn't get the chance to do. He finished counting his money, then called Walid to see if he wanted him to run any errands for him. After ending the call, he got a call from Cash. "I'll be right there," he told him, ending the call.

~ ~ ~

Supreme hooked up with Cash later that night, and to his surprise, he had the remainder of the money he owed plus more than half of the new money. Supreme had to follow him to his stash house to get it though. When they walked in, some fiends were sitting at the kitchen table about to shoot up. Supreme had to smirk when he saw that they were getting high off his product. He finally got the chance to see how the fiends reacted to the dope.

"I'll only be a minute," Cash said, walking into the other room.

"Cool!" Supreme began to say, until his cell rang. It was Walid. "Yo, bro!"

"Yo, I need you to take a trip passed Jefferson street and see if that nigga Frank is out there. I just received a call from some bitch, and she said that he's out there gambling."

"I'm gonna head over there soon as I grab this money from Cash."

"Damn, he's ready? That's what's up!" Walid replied. "Don't try to holla at bull till I get back. I just want to know where we can catch him at."

"Okay, let me handle this; then I'll go take care of that." Supreme hung up and waited for Cash to come back, before heading over to catch a thief.

"Here, Preme," Cash said, passing him an envelope full of cash.

"Yo, I need you to take a ride with me real quick. I'm trying to find that nigga Frank. He owes me some money."

"We can do that."

"Can we take your car, 'cause I don't want him to see my whip and run." He was going against everything Walid had told him. His mistake was telling Cash about the situation. He only knew him because of Walid.

"Let's go!"

~ ~ ~

They cruised down the block slowly in search of Frank, when Preme noticed a group of people huddled up near the wall playing dice. Everyone was so focused on the crap game that they didn't even notice them. Besides that, there was a black Mercedes Benz parked near them with three girls standing there talking to its occupants.

"Do you see him yet?" Cash asked.

"Nope," Supreme answered slowly.

Cash continued to drive, but they still didn't see him. He spun around the block, then came back through. This time people started to notice them driving slow.

"I don't think he's out here, Preme."

"He must have left. Damn!"

As they were approaching the end of the block again, cash hit the brakes. He locked eyes with two kids staring at them, grinning from ear to ear.

"What the fuck are they looking at?" Cash asked.

"Who?"

"Them two niggas over there!" he said, pointing in the direction where the dudes were playing dice.

This time Supreme's focus was on the two boys that continued to stare at them. Preme turned to his left just in time.

"Duck!" Supreme yelled, seeing Frank standing not even ten feet away with a long-nose revolver aimed at them.

Scurrrrrrr! Cash slammed on the gas, causing the car to peel off sluggishly.

Boom! Boom! Boom! Frank fired at them three times trying to kill them. They ducked down as one of the bullets from his gun shattered Cash's entire rearview window. Cash turned the corner just as two more shots came in their direction. *Boom! Boom!*

"Preme, you alright?"

"Yeah, just get us the fuck out of here!"

Cash almost lost control of the car trying to get away from the flying bullets, but regained control easily. Supreme glanced back to make sure they weren't being followed. The coast was clear, but his heart was still rapidly beating.

"He's gone!" Cash shouted.

"Yeah!"

"What the fuck just happened? That nigga tried to take us out. I knew I should have brought my fucking gun," Cash snapped. "I don't know why I listened to some fucking kid. You or Walid is gonna pay for my window too."

"Here, I'll pay for your window, but don't you ever talk to me like that again," Supreme replied. He peeled off six hundred dollars from the money and passed it to Cash.

"My fault, homie. That muthafucka just crossed the line shooting at me like that. I'm coming back and tearing that whole fucking block up."

"Let's get these niggas then. This muthafucka don't know who the fuck I am! He done fucked up now, trying to lay me down." Supreme contemplated calling Walid, but decided against it. This was gonna get handled tonight, and nothing was going to stop them. Cash went back to his house, then went into his room where he kept his arsenal. They strapped up, then headed back to Jefferson Street. By time they returned, the whole block was deserted. Both Supreme and Cash were hungry for revenge, but it wouldn't be tonight.

"Don't worry, that nigga will get his soon," Cash stated, dropping Supreme off at his car. "Get with me!"

"Will do!" Supreme replied, hopping in his car. When he got home, he lay across his bed, and fell asleep thinking about how his life was almost taken away from him.

~ ~ ~

The sound of his cell phone ringing woke him up from his sleep. It was his psychologist! He was about to answer it, but the ringing stopped. Thirty seconds later, it went off again. "Hello!"

"Supreme, why are you not here yet? You're late for your appointment."

He looked at the time on his phone, then jumped up off his bed, rushing to get dressed. He was over an hour late for his appointment with Karen. "I'm on my way there now," Supreme told her, then disconnected the call.

Supreme grabbed some work that he was going to drop off at one of his spots, tucked his gun in his waist, then hurried out of the house. So much had gone down last night that he decided to hide the dope in his room, because he didn't have time to run it over to the stash spot. He also hoped that he saw Frank in his travels because he wanted some payback.

While driving, he gave Walid a call to fill him in on the chain of events that took place. Walid was furious and told him that he would be back in a few hours. By the time he left from seeing Karen, his worker was ready for the new product. He headed over to the trap house to drop off the package and up his money.

"What's up, homie? Everything cool?" Supreme asked when Merv got in the car.

"Yeah, everything's cool, but I have a question for you."

"What is it, 'cause I have some shit to take care of."

"I just heard some crazy shit about that nigga Frank." Merv paused, making sure he had Supreme's attention before continuing. "I heard that he fucked you and Walid over. Why didn't you put me up on game?"

"We didn't want that shit all over the street. Then he would try to hide from us."

"I see that nigga damn near every day, Preme."

"Yeah?"

"That's not all either. He was on Jefferson street bragging to everyone that he had y'all begging for your lives."

"Begging for our lives?" Supreme asked in confusion.

"Yeah! He said the only reason he didn't pop Walid was because you was in the car. That's why he just pistol whipped him until you gave him the work."

"Are you fucking serious? That punk-ass nigga ain't do shit to us. It didn't even go down like that at all. He stole our shit but like a coward. I would have respected him more if he did do all that shit that he was talking, but instead he did some ol' sucker shit. When I catch him I'm gonna make an example out of his bitch ass, right in front of everybody," Supreme said, pissed off that he tried to play him and his man. Once Walid heard about this, he was gonna be madder than Supreme was.

"When I see bull again, I'ma put a hot one in him on the strength of him going around frauding to everybody."

"Naw, when you see him, hit my cell and I'll take care of him."

"Okay, Preme, I got you," Merv replied, getting out of the car.

Supreme headed home mad as hell. He couldn't wait to see Frank so he could bust his ass in broad daylight, in front of the world.

"These muthafuckas are going to know not to play with Preme," he said out loud to himself.

TEN

JUSTICE

"WHAT'S UP?" DONTE ASKED, talking to Dominique on his cell.

"Shit. Just having fun up in here with these niggas. This shit is jumping, baby," she said, out of breath.

"Okay, so how many people up in there? Just give me a number, niggas first."

The party had been postponed because Footie's man's release date had gotten pushed back due to a detainer. Dominique began to speak but was interrupted. Speaking to someone in the background, she could be heard telling them to hold on, that she had to take this call. She walked into the bathroom to finish her conversation.

"Ten niggas, five females."

"Have you seen any of them carrying burners?"

"No. I've felt on each and every one of those niggas too.

If they have them, they left them in the car," Dom replied.

"Okay! How is the paper looking?" he said, interrogating his girl some more.

"These niggas are throwing shit around like water. Not to mention they came stuntin' with all their jewels and other shit. They have bags and bags of money."

"Okay, check this out, baby. Unlock the back door at exactly 3:00 a.m. Then do the same for the front," Donte instructed.

"Gotcha, baby!" Dominique said, taking in his instructions while keeping an eye on the bathroom door to make sure no one was listening.

"Dom, make sure you watch yourself, because we're coming through that bitch heavy. Do you have your hammer with you?" he instinctively asked, although he knew she would have one on her.

"You already know this, baby," she assured him.

"Alright then, see ya soon, and be careful," Donte told her, then ended the call. He then turned to everybody to fill them in on what was going down. "Justice and Tank, y'all enter through the back door hard. Make sure y'all synchronize your watches so we're all on the same page."

"Say no more," Justice replied.

"Bub, once again, you gonna be the driver. Park around the corner with the van off, waiting on our call to scoop us up."

"Man, we have to teach these niggas how to drive. I'm tired of being the driver," Bub stated in frustration. He wanted to get his hands dirty.

"We all know how to drive," Justice replied, taking up for his brothers.

"I'll drive the van," Chris volunteered.

"Okay then, Bub, me and you will go through the front. There's ten niggas up in there, so if anyone acts crazy, park their asses. Tank, make sure you leave the acid and syringes at the back door. After the house is secure, we'll send Dom out back to retrieve them. Everybody wear a vest as a precaution. Justice, you can finish the game plan."

"Upon entry we need to be careful and make sure every room is secure. Cover each other's asses until all the potential threats have been neutralized," Justice said like a true leader. Donte had taken a liking to him since their last lick and knew he could handle himself.

Feeling confident that they had covered everything, Donte sparked up the loud and took a couple of puffs. He checked his watch, making sure it coordinated with everyone else's.

"Slow down and make a left in the next alley," he told Bub. "Hit the lights and park on the side street. Let's do this!"

Jumping out of the van like a specially trained SWAT team and taking their positions, each of them was ready to handle whatever was in store on the other side of the door. They hoped everything went according to plan. Donte checked his watch once again, letting everyone know it was almost showtime. As if on cue, the crew pulled their ski masks down over their faces.

"Let's get it!"

At exactly 3:00 a.m., Donte turned the knob on the front door. Finding it unlocked, he exploded through the door. Catching them by surprise, he came running through smacking anyone within his reach with the MAC-11 he was carrying.

"Get down, pussies, or lay down," Bub shouted.

As planned, they held down the entrance to the front. A couple of niggas that were sitting on the couch tried to make a run for the back door, but were met with guns to their heads. Hearing the screams over the music assured Donte that they weren't going anywhere.

One unfortunate dude that came rushing out of the room, gun in hand, caught three shots to the dome. *Bloca! Bloca! Bloca!* He was dead before he hit the ground. When Donte looked up, Bub was holding the smoking gun in his hand. "I told these niggas not to move," he stated.

Stepping over his corpse, Bub immediately went to secure the room he came out of. Upon entering the room he heard a noise in the closet. Walking over to the door and carefully opening it, he saw what appeared to be a frightened female. He dragged her out by her hair, then realized that the frightened female was his girl, Shawna. He had tried to call her before he left, but she wouldn't answer her cell phone. "Shawna?" he said, making the mistake of saying her name.

Upon hearing his voice, she immediately knew who he was behind that black ski mask. She looked up at his face in shock. "Bub, is that you?"

"Shut up, bitch! Get your ass back in the closet and be the fuck quiet." He headed back out just as Donte was entering to make sure it was clear. Without looking back he simply said, "Yeah, it's all good."

In the living room, Tank was ushering the men into the kitchen after stripping them of their clothes and possessions. He made them crawl on their hands and knees toward the back of the house. Getting irritated from the loud music, Dominique, not knowing how to operate the stereo system, walked over and unplugged it. She noticed one of the female strippers giving her a mean stare and gave her a devious smile. "Get naked, hoes. It's a cold game we're playing, but it's fair. Y'all came here to strip, so bitches do your jobs," she said.

Tired of being patient with them, Justice walked over to the nearest female, who happened to be a redbone. He violently kicked her straight in the face, knocking her teeth out. Still standing over her, he looked at the other bitches. "Get asshole naked, or join your fucking friend right here," he demanded.

Syida, who was half black and Philippine, was the first to get naked. She thought to herself that they were on some freaky shit and they could have some pussy, but they were going to pay for it with some prison time once it was all over. The rest of the girls followed suit and stripped down to nothing.

Without hesitation, Dom instructed all of them to lie flat on their stomachs with their noses touching the floor. She and Tank taped all their hands up so they would have very little resistance taping their legs and ankles as well. Then they began taping their entire heads, careful not to miss a spot. Two of them realized they were being smothered, and went crazy, causing Dom to pistol whip them unconscious. "I told you not to move," she smirked.

Walking into the kitchen, Donte observed Justice standing over one of the victims, injecting the battery acid into his neck. So was Bub. Him and Tank started helping them out while Dom kept watch just in case something went wrong. Within a matter of minutes, the only people breathing in the house were their crew.

Donte called Chris to tell him to pull up in the back in five minutes. When he looked back, Tank and Bub were placing all the possessions in plastic bags, along with the duct tape and needles. "I'm going to check around and make sure we didn't leave anything that might implicate us," Dom said.

"Okay, we'll finish up in here." While looking around, she noticed that one of the women wasn't present. There were only four lying on the floor, when in fact there should have been five. She walked into the back room where the dude tried to get the drop on them.

"This bitch done fucked up now," she whispered to herself when she heard movement coming from inside the closet. Remembering that Shawna, the light skin smart-mouth bitch, was in there earlier getting her fuck on, Dom snuck up on her. She aimed her weapon, then opened the door, firing on Shawna, who was in the corner with a coat over her face.

Dominique walked over to make sure she was dead, and noticed that she had her cell phone in her hand, which now was on the floor. Dom picked it up, then put it to her ear. Someone was on the other end, hysterically screaming. Dom quickly ended the call and ran into the other room yelling, "Let's get the fuck out of here. There was a bitch in the closet hiding, and she got a call out."

"What the fuck! Come on, let's go," Donte shouted. Hearing that, they all broke out the rear door just in time.

Chris was just pulling up with the lights out. Jumping into the van, everyone was in panic mode.

"Chris, get us the fuck out of here now," Justice screamed. He hit the gas, causing everyone to fall backward. Sirens could be heard approaching fast in the distant background as they made their way to the highway.

"Slow down some, Chris, so we don't draw no unwanted attention," Donte said, sitting back in his seat. He was furious about how that girl was able to evade a search without being noticed, but right now wasn't the time to get into it. Knowing that this fuckup could have cost them everything, he was going to make sure someone paid with their life. "I'm not gonna get into it right now, but I need to know how the hell that happened."

Sitting in the back of the van, Bub silently held his head down, while trying to conceal the tears of pain from losing Shawna, the love of his life. Right now, he was wishing she would have never been there in the first place. He could still see the scared look on her face when he opened that closet door. He had to turn his head as a tear escaped.

"Is everybody good?" Chris asked, looking in the rearview mirror.

"Yeah, we're all good, bro. Let's get back to the spot so we can count this merchandise," Justice replied, tapping him on the shoulder.

Bub sat in the back looking at each member of his crew. He made a silent vow to avenge his girlfriend's death someway, somehow. The whole time he was thinking that, Justice was sitting there remembering that it was him that said the room was clear, and was trying to figure out the connection between the two.

ELEVEN

SUPREME

SUPREME AND WALID HAD received a call from Merv around eight o'clock that night, saying that Frank was on the block playing craps with a couple of niggas. They told him they were on their way to scoop him up. When they got there, Merv was sitting on the steps in front of his crib. Merv didn't know who was in the car because the windows were tinted, so he immediately put his guard up by placing his hand on his gun. When Walid rolled the window down, he relaxed.

"What's up, nigga?" Supreme asked, as Merv grabbed the door handle, then hopped in the car.

"What's good fellas! I didn't know who the fuck you were," he said. "I've done so much dirt, I thought someone was trying to creep me."

"You sure you want to roll with us?" Walid asked, pulling out of the parking spot.

"What, me not wanting to roll with my peoples? Nigga,

you sound stupid. I wouldn't miss this for the world. You know this is what I live for. Here, let me sync my phone so I can play my shit." After syncing his phone, Merv found the song he was looking for and hit the play button. He sat there in a zone, with his eyes closed, bopping his head to the beat. As soon as the song went off, he played it again.

♫ *I'll box ya fucking head off. Who gone knock the kid off? None of y'all, which one of y'all come try me. I'll body lil homeboy, silence that sound boy. Come challenge me please, I promise you a homi'* ♫

Beanie Sigel and Peedi Crakk filled the speakers. "This right here is my riding music! This is what I listen to when I'm preparing to put in work." The whole time Merv kept his eyes closed, Walid nor Supreme said anything to disturb him. He pulled out his rubber grip P89, then checked to see if one was in the chamber. He still never said a word. He just continued to bounce to the music.

"Is that them right there?" Supreme asked anxiously. He wanted to get Frank so bad that his trigger finger was itching.

"That's that niggas car, but I don't know if he's in it or not," Merv replied.

Two dudes were standing next to another car talking to the occupant inside. They're laughing and playing around, not paying any attention to their surroundings. One of them kept opening the passenger's door back and forth.

"Pull a little closer," Merv told Walid. "The tall one looks like it could be him."

"That's not him! That nigga has braids, and he's shorter," Walid replied. "I thought your man said he was out here?"

"He might be in that car, 'cause they're not out playing craps anymore," Supreme said, watching it very close. Merv didn't say another word for the next ten minutes. He just continued listening to the music, letting his mind take him to another place. The kill zone!

"Merv, what's up? You're quiet as shit back there. You good?"

"Yeah, I'm good! I'm just waiting for the word so we

can get into some gunplay. I know one thing, we have to hurry up. We can't sit out here all night waiting on this clown. This block is hot as hell at night. The cops stay coming through here. That's why them try niggas make their money on the block during the day, and go to them at night."

Just as he said that, the interior light to the car came on. The driver door opened up. A girl with skintight jeans stepped out laughing. Her ass was so fat that half of it was still resting on the seat. She walked around to the passenger side. Then her and the dude started play fighting. He lifted her up by her ass and began pumping on her like a maniac. Then the passenger door opened up, and a second girl jumped out. She stood there laughing at her friend as the dude started smacking her on the ass.

"Damn, this nigga must have stepped off 'cause he's not out here, and it's starting to piss me the fuck off," Walid said angrily.

"Right there!"

They looked over toward the corner store, and Frank

came strolling out talking to someone on his phone. Walid's face turned stone cold.

"Finally, this pussy comes out of hiding," Supreme said, cocking his gun.

"Chill, put it away for a minute. Here come the cops!"

"Where?"

"Coming down the block!"

"Turn the car off," Merv blurted out. The cop car eased through the block slowly. Walid and Supreme scooted down in their seats, even though the windows were tinted, so the cops couldn't see their shadow. The police car drove right past them, then turned the corner. "I think we should hurry up and get the hell out of here before they come back. Our window of opportunity is fading fast."

"I'm not leaving until that nigga's body is somewhere stinking," Supreme stated.

"That's the other nigga that was out there grinning at us when that shit popped off," Merv said, pointing to the dude that just stepped out of the backseat.

"Oh yeah, his fucking cheerleader!"

"Man, fuck this. Pull up beside them," Supreme told Walid.

"Chill, dickhead. Those girls out there, they don't have shit to do with it."

"Them bitches shouldn't be out here!" Supreme shouted. "That nigga disrespected us, and I didn't sit out here all this time for nothing."

"Let's chill for a few more minutes, Preme. Let the girls leave first," Walid suggested. "If they're still here in a few minutes, then fuck them."

As if the girls recognized the threat, they got back in the car and started the engine. The dude with the braids shook Frank and the other dude's hand, then jumped in the back. As soon as they pulled off, Supreme's adrenaline started to kick in. "You ready, Merv?"

Without responding, Merv clicked the safety off his weapon, then gave Supreme a head nod. Walid slowly pulled out of the parking spot, checking his rearview mirror to make sure the street was clear. Frank and his man looked up at the car, but it was too late.

Boom! Boom! Boc! Boc! Boc! Boc! The shots hit them simultaneously in the chest area. The impact knocked them both in the air, then to the ground. Frank's head hit the steps with a loud thump. The other guy's body ricocheted, and he splattered face-first onto the asphalt.

"Agghhh!" Frank screamed, holding his chest.

Supreme jumped out, with Merv right behind him. Merv finished the dude off with a shot to the dome, while Supreme walked over to where Frank was squirming on the ground. He bent down over him, and the look in his eyes was like a man possessed. He grabbed Frank by the shoulders and turned him over. He dug into his pockets, pulling out a wad of cash. "I believe this belongs to me. You shouldn't have never stole from us, nigga," he whispered.

"Pleeeaaase, don't kill me."

Supreme stood straight up, then emptied the rest of his clip into him, his body absorbing every bullet. Supreme was still pulling the trigger even after the bullets were gone. Walid had to jump out of the car and yell at Supreme to snap him out of the psychotic stage he was in. "Let's go, Preme!" He still stood there as if he had more bullets that needed to be discharged from his weapon. "Preme, I said let's go." This time Walid grabbed him by the arm, pushing him toward the car.

Supreme hopped in the backseat, Merv in the front. "Motherfucker," Preme shouted. "Did you see the way his body bounced off that ground? Wait until niggas hear about this on the news. I bet nobody else tries to disrespect us. Speaking of disrespect, I don't like being called a dickhead." Merv never responded, he just turned his music back on as they drove away.

Twenty minutes later, they pulled up to Merv's car. He shook their hands, then opened the door. "Good looking on that situation," Walid said.

"No problem, Walid. Like I told you before, if you need me, I'm just a call away," he said, walking toward his car.

"Hold up a second yo!" Preme yelled.

"What's up?" Merv replied, rolling the window down.

"How much do we owe you?" Supreme asked, pulling out the wad of cash he took off of Frank.

"Come on, man, don't insult me like that," he replied. "I done that from the heart."

"I feel you, but you gotta charge me something. Business, never personal, bro."

"Seriously, I'm good, bro, for real."

"Charge me something," Preme demanded. He just felt like he had to give him something for moving out like that. Plus, he didn't want him to ever try to hold that over his head. "How much, bro? Just name it."

"Just make me a part of the team. I'm an asset. You need a nigga like me on your team."

"You're right. Come to the trap house tomorrow and we'll talk." Merv gave him a nod, then pulled off. He hopped back in the car with Walid, and he drove him home.

They sat outside counting the money they took from

Frank. In total, it was over twenty racks. Walid told him to hold on to it just in case he had to bail one of the workers out. He figured that it wouldn't be their money being spent. "I'll hit you up tomorrow," Supreme said, heading into the house.

He went straight up to his room to put the money with the work that he had stashed. When he looked inside the shoebox, it was empty. He couldn't believe his eyes and thought maybe he stuck it in one of the other boxes. "What the fuck?" he mumbled, tearing his closet up, trying to find the dope.

"Looking for this?" he heard someone say behind him. When he turned around, his adoptive mom was standing there, holding the drugs. "Give me a reason why I shouldn't be standing here with the police, ready to haul your behind off to jail?"

Supreme was speechless at the moment. He didn't have an answer that would be good enough to get him out of this predicament. The look of hurt and disappointment on her face said it all. "I'm sorry, but I was tired of not having my own stuff. I can't keep depending on you," he said.

"Supreme, we are your family, and we took you in to provide for you. I guess we're not doing enough for you, which means we're not doing our job as parents. So you have three options, and that's it. You can go back to that home, take this stuff and flush it down the toilet and we'll never have this conversation again, or take it and get the hell out of my house, 'cause no child of mine is gonna be out here selling drugs."

"I can't just flush that stuff down the toilet."

"Well then I guess your choice was made then. I want you and this stuff," she said, throwing it at him, "out of my house tonight."

"Fuck it then. I don't need to be here," Supreme snapped. He picked up the package and started gathering some clothes, throwing them in a plastic bag. "I'm never going back to no fucking boys home."

Francis couldn't believe how crazy he was acting. Larry

heard the commotion and got out of bed to see what was going on. When he walked into the room, he noticed how upset his wife was. Even Elizabeth came out of her room after hearing all the yelling.

"What's going on in here?" Larry asked.

"Why don't you ask your wife, since she has all the answers. I'm out of here." Supreme pushed past everyone and headed down the stairs.

Elizabeth followed behind him, catching up to him before he walked out the door. "Preme, what happened, and where are you going?"

"Your mom found my dope. I should have let you hold it for me. Now she's kicking me out if I don't flush it down the toilet."

"Where will you go?" she asked again, knowing that throwing the drugs away was not an option for him.

"I'll be alright. If you need anything, you have my number, just call me, okay?" he said, giving his adoptive sister a hug. They had become close since he moved in. He did anything for her, and she for him. She cried as she watched him walk down the street and get into his car. She secretly loved Supreme, but knew they could never be together.

"Hey, what are you doing sexy?" Supreme probed, sitting in his car. He had called Kreasha to check on her. They hadn't seen each other in two days, ever since that shit happened with Frank.

"Nothing, just came in the house. What you doing?"

"Sitting in my car. My adoptive parents found my stash and kicked me out."

"Why don't you come over here and stay the night? My mom's not gonna care. She's probably somewhere getting high with her friends anyway."

"You sure?"

"Yes, plus I need some dick anyway."

"Oh really," he smiled. "Are you coming or not?" she purposefully whined.

"Yeah, I'm on my way," he told her, ending the call.

He was gonna call Walid, but since he was chilling with his girl, he decided to wait until the next morning. He was definitely going to have to find a place to stay soon, but for now Kreasha's crib would have to do.

~ ~ ~

It had been almost three weeks since the fallout between Supreme and his adoptive parents. He hadn't talked to them since. It didn't matter though because he and Walid were supplying the Tri-State area with dope, so they were making a lot of money.

Supreme and Kreasha decided to get a crib in Philly together. He had to put it in her name because he wasn't old enough yet. They were lying in bed when he received a call from one of his workers. "Yizzo!"

"Preme, I hate to call you this early, but shit has been popping out here."

"So what's up?"

"I've been out here all night, and we're getting dry, bro. Get up and bring me some more so I don't run out. It's payday, and you know what that means."

"You gonna have to give me about an hour or so. I have to call Walid to meet me there. I gave everything I had out last night. He has the new work, and we was supposed to meet up this morning so we could cut and bag it up."

"Damn, can you make it here sooner than that? It will be gone soon."

"I'ma call him right now and tell him you need it. Don't worry, we'll be there before you're out, okay?" Supreme told him.

He hung up and immediately called Walid. He told Supreme that he would take care of it right now since he was only twenty minutes away. Supreme was relieved that he didn't have to rush now. He let Walid know he would meet up with him in an hour so they could cut and bag up the work. Next, he took a quick shower, then put on some shorts until he found something to wear.

"Babe, I'm gonna go shopping with my girlfriends today. Can I get some money?" Kreasha asked seductively. She had found the gym bag full of cash and wanted some.

"Damn, we trying to make a major move today, baby. You may have to wait."

Not one to be detoured from her quest, Kreasha walked up to Supreme then kissed him passionately while rubbing her hand over his stomach and down the shorts he was wearing. She grabbed his dick and started rubbing it. "You need me to handle this for you?" she asked. She didn't even wait for a reply. She dropped down to her knees and started from the base of his dick. Licking and sucking her way up to the head of his shaft, feeling the veins pulse from his dick in her hot mouth, she wrapped her sexy lips around him, taking in as much as her mouth would allow while rubbing his balls. Looking up at him with her sexy hazel eyes, she moaned.

Supreme grabbed her by her long hair and started fucking her mouth, not caring that she was gagging. He released his load of hot sperm all down her throat. Not finished, she stood up and pulled him toward the bed. They quickly stripped all their clothes off, then got in bed. Kissing her on her soft breasts, he made his way down to her shaven pussy, which was now dripping wet. "Oh shit!" Kreasha moaned. Sliding his long hot tongue into her pussy, licking and sucking on her sensitive clit, made her cum fast and hard. Her clit quivered around his lips.

"Turn around," Supreme ordered, lifting up off of her. Knowing he liked to fuck her doggy style, she willingly obliged. Smacking her on the ass, he rubbed his fingers in and out of her pussy, sliding her juices up to her asshole. He slid his dick into her ass with a vengeful thrust, fucking her like it was his last chance to bust a nut. He pulled her hair and pounded her asshole at the same time. "You like this shit, don't you?" he smirked.

"Yessssss, Preme, don't stop," she replied, bucking back.

Feeling his nut about to bust, he pulled out and shot his stream of cum all over her perfectly round ass. Collapsing on the bed, exhausted from the ass fucking, he rolled over and relaxed for a few minutes. "How much do you need to go shopping?" he asked, defeated. She smiled to herself, knowing that she had once again succeeded in getting what she wanted from him. It was time to tear the mall down.

TWELVE

JUSTICE

JUSTICE HAD BEEN SPENDING a lot of time with Gabby lately. He bought her anything she wanted, and in return, she gave him what he wanted. Tank and Chris thought she was using him at first, but then realized they were truly in love. Malik told the boys to take a walk with him so they could talk. Soon as they got to the neighborhood park, Tank sparked up the loud that he rolled up before leaving the house. "I wanted to drop some more knowledge on you fellas before y'all go out on another lick. First and foremost, y'all are young men, so the decisions you make, just remember that they don't just affect you. They also affect the people around you."

"Malik, I know what you saying, and I would never bring our drama back home with us. That's why we do our dirt in other cities where no one knows us," Justice shot back.

"I understand that, Just. Basically these are your brothers

right here," Malik started, pointing to Tank and Chris. "That's all you have! Fake friends are going to come and go. They may even do anything in their power to tear y'all apart. Never let anyone cause friction between you. Are you listening to me, Chris?"

Chris was looking down the street at a bunch of girls arguing. He turned back toward Malik and nodded his head. "Yeah," he answered.

"Anyway, as I was saying, take care of each other out here. People are gonna try to take you out for trying to take what they worked for, so you better be ready to bust your gun on sight. Blood is thicker than water and always will be. If any of you ever need me, I'm only a phone call away." Justice understood what he was trying to say, and made sure he locked it in his brain. It would surely become useful soon. "Good talk, Malik," he said.

"I'm starving. Let's go eat," Malik replied.

~ ~ ~

Later that night Justice and Tank were on their way to

meet up with Donte. Tank had told him earlier about another lick that was in the making, and they were about to go over the plan. Donte and Dominique were sitting at the kitchen table when they walked in, counting stacks of money. "Don't y'all think this is too fast to be hitting another crib? The streets are talking, and if they're talking, what you think the police are doing?" Dominique asked.

"Man, fuck the pigs. They can get it too," Justice replied.

"Fuck you mean by that? We can't go starting no fucking war with the fucking police."

"Chill out, y'all!" Donte said, cutting them off. "Let's stay focused here. So, Tank, what's up with these niggas?"

"The bitch said they got shit on lock in Philly and Delaware. Their main spot is in Philly, and he took her there a few times. She said only him and his partner go there, so it will be easy to get in and out. How do you want to play this?" Tank asked.

"This source of yours is reliable, right?" Donte said.

"Definitely! She has been getting close to the nigga for a

couple of weeks now, and he wants her to help him count the money tonight on some bragging shit. She seen him throw bags of money in his trunk a couple of times when they were together."

"That's how niggas always fuck up, flashing all their money in these bitches faces. They don't know who they're showing it off to," Justice replied, shaking his head.

Dominique sat there listening to them talk while thinking how she never heard anything about this dude. She had always gotten the rundown on niggas getting money, but there was something fishy about this one. "I still think it's too early to go at them," Dom continued to object.

"I think Dom is right though. We need to fall back for a minute and get to know who we're dealing with first, instead of going in blind," Donte suggested.

"Whatever, man," Tank said. "What's up with all this money here?"

"Half of it belongs to y'all," Donte said, pushing it over toward them. "That is the money from the drugs we got rid of. Some people I knew from out Harrisburg took them off our hands." Justice and Tank smiled at the money sitting in front of them. They never saw so much money in their entire life. Instead of it making Tank want to chill, it only made him want to get more. He was going to talk Justice into doing the lick without Donte. He figured if they did it alone, it would be more for them and they would be cutting out the middle man.

"Don't forget to give Chris his share," Donte said, grabbing himself a drink.

"I won't! Let's go celebrate our accomplishments!" Justice told them.

"Yeah, I want to go to a strip club. Neither one of us has ever been there," Tank said, throwing some money in the air. They laughed at him making it rain in the kitchen like he was already there. Dom started acting like she was the dancer, picking the money up.

"Y'all coming with us?" asked Justice.

"No, we have some other shit to take care of. Have fun

for us," Dom replied, interrupting their little celebration. She walked next to Donte and squeezed his dick. "Let's go, daddy!"

Nothing else needed to be said. They all shook hands, and then Justice and Tank left. Justice had his girl's car, so they headed over to Haks strip club to have some fun. A vehicle was one of the things on his list of things to get. He decided he would look for one tomorrow.

~ ~ ~

They pulled up in front of the club and parked. There were a lot of cars out, which meant the club was crowded. As they walked inside, their questions were answered immediately by all the people sitting around the stage and bar area. "I can't believe we got in here so easy. They didn't even ask us for ID," Justice said.

"Fuck it, we here now, so let's enjoy ourselves," Tank replied.

They sat at the bar like they were twenty-one, and waited

to be served. Justice's attention was drawn to the center of the stage. Right in the middle was a big black bathtub. There were four naked women and some dude inside that they picked from the crowd. Two of the women were tearing his clothes off of him. One was a petite black girl, and the other was a thick white girl with the fattest ass he had ever seen.

After taking his clothes off, they licked his entire body down. They dropped to their knees and then took turns sucking his dick. They alternated, taking two licks apiece. After the second lick, they passionately tongue kissed while the head of his dick was in both of their mouths. After the wet sloppy kissing, they both finished pleasing the birthday dude. The black girl continued to suck him off, while the white girl licked his balls.

The other two women were Asian. They looked like they could have been twins. Both of them were extremely thin, with enormous breasts. They were putting on a show of their own. One was standing up showering with her legs slightly spread apart, while the other one was on her knees submissively licking her pussy. Her tiny body began trembling uncontrollably as she reached her climax.

Justice sat there, mouth wide open as he watched the show. He was snapped out of his trance when Tank playfully punched him in the arm. "You good, bro?"

"Yeah, I'm straight. What's up?" Justice replied.

"Listen, I'm trying to tell you, bro, we could do this shit by ourselves and split the money three ways instead of five," Tank said while throwing dollars on stage at the dancer.

"Who are they?"

"Like I told Donte, I don't know who they are. All I know is that the chick Gina be hanging with one of my lil bitches, and I heard them talking." Just hearing Gina's name made Justice's mood change. He wondered why he always mentioned her. It was Tank who first told him she was out there tricking with niggas and he should watch out.

"Fuck that bitch," Justice snapped. "Can you contact that bitch now and set something up?"

"I can check right now if you want."

"Yeah, see what's up! I'm always down for some free money," Justice replied. Tank stepped off so he could go somewhere quiet to call his lil bitch. Justice sat at the bar, when he noticed a waitress approaching him. She had a set of titties that were round with thick, dark nipples. She was caramel complected, with long curly hair that came down past her slim waistline. She had green eyes and pretty white teeth.

"Hello, may I take your order?" she asked.

"Yeah, let me get a cranberry and orange juice."

"Okay, give me a second." As she walked away, Justice couldn't help but notice her fat ass. It was nice and firm, and it swallowed the thong she was wearing. She unexpectedly turned around and caught him staring at her. The chick gave him a smile and then continued to the other side of the bar. As she mixed a drink for another customer, Justice watched her ass jiggle while she shook the drink extra fast. She knew she had his undivided attention, so she teased him.

A few minutes later she returned and placed his drink on

the counter. "Two dollars please!" she shouted over the loud music. Justice stared at her titties while passing her a ten-dollar bill. She gave him back his change. As he tried to pull his hand back, she grabbed hold of both of them. She placed one on her firm breast, and the other she slowly rubbed on her clean-shaven pussy.

He slid a finger in between her pussy lips, searching for her clit. He then rubbed it gently between his thumb and pointer finger. She started grinding on his hand as she sang along with the August Alsina song that blasted through the speakers. Justice sneakily slid his finger into her hot pussy. To his surprise, she didn't pull away. Instead, she arched her back and began to fuck his finger, pumping faster with each stroke. "Mmmmmmm," she moaned.

She applied more pressure as she ground with short, deep pumps. Justice slid his finger further inside her. She was so wet and deep that her juices flowed down his finger each time he pulled out of her. She closed her eyes and leaned her head back. Suddenly she grabbed his hand with a tight grip, and slowly pulled his finger out of her pussy. She put his hand close to her face, then kissed the palm, then licked his index finger like it was a dick.

She instructed him to come closer, which he did without a word. The sweet smell of Victoria's Secret's Strawberries and Crème filled his nostrils. She began to stroke Justice's ear with her moist tongue. His dick was so hard that it felt like it was going to bust through his jeans. "You touched it, so tip it," she whispered in his ear.

Justice reached inside his pocket and pulled out two twenty dollar bills. Before he could pass them to her, she stuck her hand down his pants and grabbed his balls. She gently squeezed them, then slid her hand over, grabbing the head of his dick, massaging it. As soon as she felt him about to bust in his pants, she moved her hand faster. Justice shot his load all over her hand and inside his pants. She gave him some napkins to wipe himself, then took the money out of his hand. "Thank you," she mouthed, walking into the back to clean up.

"I set everything up for tomorrow," Tank said, walking up behind Justice as he was wiping his pants off.

"Should I ask?"

"No!" Justice answered, giving him a crazy look.

"You ready to get up out of here?"

"Yeah! Do not say anything to nobody about what we're gonna do. Not even Chris, okay?"

"I hear you," Tank said as they headed out of the club. Once Justice dropped off Tank, he took Gabby her car back. She was standing outside waiting for him. She wanted him to come in, but he lied so she didn't see the stain in his pants. He went home thinking about the girl at the club. He would definitely be seeing her again.

THIRTEEN

SUPREME

"WHAT'S UP, WALID?" SUPREME said, walking into the kitchen. He was carrying a bag of money that he had just picked up from the trap houses.

"What's up, lil homie!" he replied, looking up momentarily from the table where he was bagging up dope. Walid respected Supreme because he was about his business, and he saw so much of himself in him. They were like a two-man wrecking crew, who were starting to have shit on lock.

He watched as Supreme dumped the money out on the counter. "I gave them all the work I had left in the car. When we finish bagging up, we have to drop some more off 'cause I know they will probably run out in a day or so. It's the beginning of the month and the busiest. You want me to count this or help you bag up?"

"It don't matter, Preme, whatever you want to do. Matter of fact, you can help me so we can hurry up and get the rest out on the street," Walid replied.

Supreme pulled up a chair and sat at the table. Once he put on some rubber gloves and a face mask, he started bagging up the heroin. Rick Ross and Meek Mill played on the PS4. They both bobbed their heads as "I'm a Boss" filled the room, until his cell phone rang.

"Yo who this?" Walid said, getting up from the table.

"Damn, you didn't save my number in your phone? I must not be on your must-see list," the caller replied. "You don't remember me?"

"Listen, shorty," he blurted out, irritated. "I'm kind of busy right now. I fuck a lot of bitches, so it's hard for me to remember people."

"Well did any of them bitches make you cum in two minutes from the best head in your life?"

"Oh shit, super head. What's up, ma?" He smiled thinking about the last time he saw her.

"By, boy!" she smirked. "Anyway, I'm trying to come see your sexy ass. What you doing today?"

"Oh, so you trying to come eat this dick up again huh?"

"As long as you cut that check, I'm down for whatever," she shot back.

"I got you, shorty! I'm really busy right now though. How about you come to the crib at eight o'clock tonight?"

"That's cool! I hope you ready."

Walid ended the call without a response.

It took them about three hours to bag up enough for all the trap houses. "Let's hurry up and drop this shit off. That bitch I told you about with the vicious head game is coming through tonight. You have to see her and get a sample of her work," Walid stated, heading toward the door.

"You crazy, bro!" Supreme told him, getting in the passenger seat.

"Preme, I'm dead serious. You gonna fall in love with that shit," he said, laughing.

They delivered the work, stopped and got something to eat, then headed back to the crib to chill. Supreme told his girl he would most likely be home late because they had to stay out tonight, and she understood without complaining. They both sat on the couch, playing NBA2K.

~ ~ ~

"Hey, Walid," Gina said as she entered his house.

Supreme looked up to see for the first time the chick Walid had been talking about. He looked at the skirt she had on and had to admit that her body was tight. When he stood up to get a better look and Gina saw him, she almost pissed on herself. Walid saw her reaction and figured they must have met before.

"I'm gonna go take a quick shower. Make yourself comfortable until I finish," Walid replied, heading upstairs. Him and Supreme had set that up to see if she would start the party up while he was upstairs.

"What are you doing here, Justice?" Gina said, staring at him confused.

Supreme's heart stopped at the mention of his brother's name. He walked over to where Gina was standing, because he thought he heard her wrong. "Who did you just call me?"

Just then, Gina noticed the long braids tucked perfectly up under the hat he was wearing. It was then that she realized that it wasn't Justice. *OMG, they look just alike*, she thought to herself. "Nothing! You look just like someone I used to know," she finally replied.

"What name did you just say?" he asked again, more aggressively.

"It doesn't matter, he's just an old friend. Nobody important!"

Not trying to play any more games, Supreme gripped her up by the shoulders and backed her up against the wall. "What fucking name did you just say?"

"Get off me! You're hurting my arms," she squealed. "I said Justice. Damn, it's not that deep."

"It is that fucking deep. Take me to my fucking brother," Supreme said with a deadly look in his eyes.

FOURTEEN

JUSTICE

JUSTICE AND TANK PARKED around the corner from the house they were about to run up in. They both checked the magazines on their weapons, making sure they were full, then finished the loud that they had been smoking on the way there.

"You sure this shit is official?" Justice asked, as they walked down the block.

"You know I trust you, so whatever we got to do I have your back. I just hope this bitch you talked to gave you some good information."

"Bro when have you ever known me to do some dumb shit when it comes to getting at some bread? M-O-B, Preme."

"Money over bitches," they both said simultaneously, nodding their heads in agreement.

"You know what, bro, you're right. Maybe I was just tripping 'cause I feel like something is gonna go wrong,"

Justice said.

"What, you wanted Donte and them to roll out with us? We got this, bro. Nothing's gonna go wrong because it's only two niggas up in there." Tank had received the text earlier, letting him know that there were only two people there.

"Let's get this fucking money, bro."

The plan was to run up in there and take the money and work. They were going to tie both of them up, but only if they didn't try to draw on them. Hopefully this time they wouldn't have to kill anyone. Tank texted his chick fifteen minutes ago telling her to leave the crib before they got there.

"This is the address right here," Tank stated, looking at his phone. They rolled the ski masks over their faces and pulled their guns out. Just as Tank's chick stated, the front door was unlocked.

"You ready?"

"On three," Justice said, cocking his gun. "One, two, three . . ."

FIFTEEN

GINA HAD NO CHOICE but to break down and tell Supreme about her so-called relationship with his brother. She even told him about how she was accused of being a whore. Supreme actually believed that part because she was just about to probably fuck him and his mans.

"I'll give you his address, but I'm not going over there," she said.

"You're going to take me to my brother," Supreme said, pulling his gun out.

He was really scaring the shit out of her now. She didn't know what he would do next, so she agreed, hoping he would put the gun in his hand away.

"I will go with you and stay in the car. Can I at least tell Walid I'm going with you?"

Before Supreme could respond, the front door flew open, and two men wearing ski masks busted in, guns in hand.

"Get the fuck on the floor," one of them shouted.

Thinking quickly, Supreme grabbed Gina to use as a shield, then pulled her close to him, behind the wall. He already had his own gun out, so he pointed it at her head. "You niggas picked the wrong fucking house to rob."

Justice couldn't believe his eyes. He knew he just didn't see his twin brother and his old chick duck behind that wall. He looked at Tank with a confused expression on his face. "What the fuck is going on?" he asked. Tank shrugged his shoulders and started walking toward the area where Supreme and Gina were, aiming his gun. Justice grabbed his arm. "Chill the fuck out, that dude is my brother."

Supreme was standing there debating if he should just go out in a blaze of glory, but the other peeps weren't moving. It all made sense to him now. "Bitch, you set us up, didn't you?"

Gina didn't reply. She just stood there in a hysterical trance, wondering what was about to happen to her. She wasn't ready to die.

"Somebody please help me," Gina screamed.

"Shut up!" Supreme smacked her over the face with the butt of his gun, then slowly moved from behind the wall, with Gina in front of him, the gun pointed at her head. "Drop your guns, or I'ma give this bitch a wig shot."

When Tank saw the gun aimed at her head, he regretted ever setting up the whole thing. He wished he would have listened to Donte. What fucked him up even more was that the nigga holding the gun looked exactly like Justice.

"It's me, bro," Justice said, lowering his gun and pulling his ski mask off. When Supreme saw his brother's face, a million emotions shot through him. He was happy, mad, and confused. He didn't know what to do, or how to feel at that moment. It took every fiber in his body not to drop his gun and embrace his brother, but right now he had to stand his ground. He had no idea what was going on.

"Aye, big bro!" Supreme said with a sinister laugh. "Shit changed. We ain't babies no more. I only love the streets, so drop the guns or I'm gonna kill this scheming bitch." He thought Justice still had love for Gina, so he tried using her to his advantage to defuse the situation.

Justice looked Gina dead in the eyes. "I don't give a fuck about that bitch, kill her ass."

When Tank heard Justice say that, he knew he had to do something, and fast. He stepped out in front of Justice, then tossed his gun on the floor. "Aye, Justice, this your brother, dawg? It was just a big misunderstanding. Let's be out."

"You trippin', nigga. Shit can't go back to normal now," Justice replied, never taking his eyes off of his brother.

Tank looked over to Supreme and tried to reason with him. "Just let her go, man. We didn't know it was you."

That seemed like the reasonable thing to do, Preme thought, but somebody needed to pay for trying to rob him. "If I let her go, it will be her hitting the ground from catching a hot one to the dome."

"Come on, man, you don't have to do this," Tank pleaded.

Out of the corner of his eye, Supreme noticed Walid

creeping down the steps with an assault rifle cocked and ready to go. Knowing that he had the upper hand now, he pushed Gina on the ground, and then looked at Justice.

"Sorry we had to meet like this, bro."

Boom! Boom! Boom!!!!

Coming Soon:

Supreme and Justice II: Hold Court on the Streets

Text Good2Go at 31996 to receive new release updates via text message

BOOKS BY GOOD2GO AUTHORS

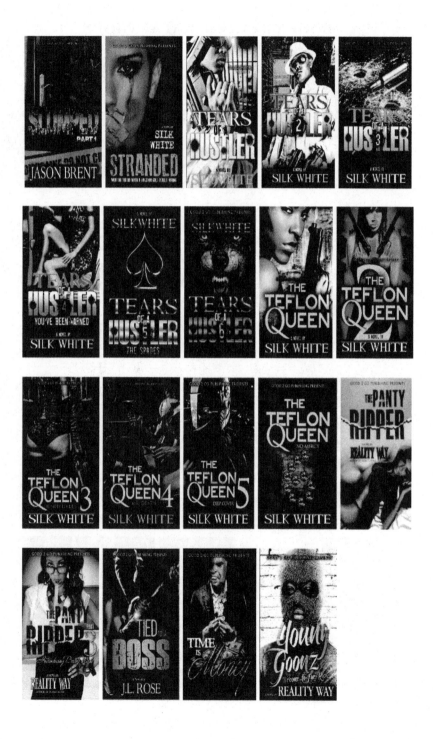

GOOD 2 GO FILMS PRESENTS

WRONG PLACE WRONG TIME WEB SERIES

**NOW AVAILABLE ON
GOOD2GOFILMS.COM & YOUTUBE
SUBSCRIBE TO THE CHANNEL**

THE HAND I WAS DEALT WEB SERIES
NOW AVAILABLE ON YOUTUBE!

SEASON TWO NOW AVAILABLE
NOW AVAILABLE ON YOUTUBE!

THE HACKMAN
NOW AVAILABLE ON YOUTUBE!

To order books, please fill out the order form below:
To order films please go to **www.good2gofilms.com**

Name:_____

Address:_____

City: _____ State: _____ Zip Code: _____

Phone:_____

Email:_____

Method of Payment: Check   VISA   MASTERCARD

Credit Card#:_____

Name as it appears on card: _____

Signature: _____

Item Name	Price	Qty	Amount
48 Hours to Die – Silk White	$14.99		
A Hustler's Dream - Ernest Morris	$14.99		
A Hustler's Dream 2 - Ernest Morris	$14.99		
Bloody Mayhem Down South	$14.99		
Business Is Business – Silk White	$14.99		
Business Is Business 2 – Silk White	$14.99		
Business Is Business 3 – Silk White	$14.99		
Childhood Sweethearts – Jacob Spears	$14.99		
Childhood Sweethearts 2 – Jacob Spears	$14.99		
Childhood Sweethearts 3 - Jacob Spears	$14.99		
Childhood Sweethearts 4 - Jacob Spears	$14.99		
Flipping Numbers – Ernest Morris	$14.99		
Flipping Numbers 2 – Ernest Morris	$14.99		
He Loves Me, He Loves You Not - Mychea	$14.99		
He Loves Me, He Loves You Not 2 - Mychea	$14.99		
He Loves Me, He Loves You Not 3 - Mychea	$14.99		
He Loves Me, He Loves You Not 4 – Mychea	$14.99		
He Loves Me, He Loves You Not 5 – Mychea	$14.99		
Lord of My Land – Jay Morrison	$14.99		
Lost and Turned Out – Ernest Morris	$14.99		
Married To Da Streets – Silk White	$14.99		
M.E.R.C. - Make Every Rep Count Health and Fitness	$14.99		
My Besties – Asia Hill	$14.99		
My Besties 2 – Asia Hill	$14.99		
My Besties 3 – Asia Hill	$14.99		
My Besties 4 – Asia Hill	$14.99		
My Boyfriend's Wife - Mychea	$14.99		
My Boyfriend's Wife 2 – Mychea	$14.99		
Naughty Housewives – Ernest Morris	$14.99		
Naughty Housewives 2 – Ernest Morris	$14.99		
Naughty Housewives 3 – Ernest Morris	$14.99		
Naughty Housewives 4 – Ernest Morris	$14.99		

Never Be The Same – Silk White	$14.99		
Stranded – Silk White	$14.99		
Slumped – Jason Brent	$14.99		
Supreme & Justice	$14.99		
Tears of a Hustler - Silk White	$14.99		
Tears of a Hustler 2 - Silk White	$14.99		
Tears of a Hustler 3 - Silk White	$14.99		
Tears of a Hustler 4- Silk White	$14.99		
Tears of a Hustler 5 – Silk White	$14.99		
Tears of a Hustler 6 – Silk White	$14.99		
The Panty Ripper - Reality Way	$14.99		
The Panty Ripper 3 – Reality Way	$14.99		
The Solution – Jay Morrison	$14.99		
The Teflon Queen – Silk White	$14.99		
The Teflon Queen 2 – Silk White	$14.99		
The Teflon Queen 3 – Silk White	$14.99		
The Teflon Queen 4 – Silk White	$14.99		
The Teflon Queen 5 – Silk White	$14.99		
The Teflon Queen 6 - Silk White	$14.99		
The Vacation – Silk White	$14.99		
Tied To A Boss - J.L. Rose	$14.99		
Tied To A Boss 2 - J.L. Rose	$14.99		
Tied To A Boss 3 - J.L. Rose	$14.99		
Tied To A Boss 4 - J.L. Rose	$14.99		
Time Is Money - Silk White	$14.99		
Two Mask One Heart – Jacob Spears and Trayvon Jackson	$14.99		
Two Mask One Heart 2 – Jacob Spears and Trayvon Jackson	$14.99		
Two Mask One Heart 3 – Jacob Spears and Trayvon Jackson	$14.99		
Wrong Place Wrong Time	$14.99		
Young Goonz – Reality Way	$14.99		
Young Legend – J.L. Rose	$14.99		
Subtotal:			
Tax:			
Shipping (Free) U.S. Media Mail:			
Total:			

Make Checks Payable To:
Good2Go Publishing
7311 W Glass Lane,
Laveen, AZ 85339